Voyeurs of Death

By

Shaun Jeffrey

Doorways Publications

Paranoid, Sin Eater, Envy and Dark Inside are original, previously unpublished stories.

"The Flibbertigibbet" originally published in DeathGrip: Legacy of Terror 2003 and later reprinted in Dark Tales 2005

"The Watchers" originally published in Dark Discoveries Volume 2, Issue 2 2005

"The Tunnel" originally published in Hauntings 2004 Cyber-pulp Press

"The Quilters of Thurmond" originally published in Grotesque #3 1993

"Voyeurs of Death" originally published in Black Tears #7 1995

"Life Cycle" originally published in Surreal Magazine #1 2005

"Clockwork" originally published in Wicked Karnival #7 2006

"Venetian Kiss" originally published in Monsters Ink 2005 Cyber-pulp Press

"Peacock Lawn" originally published in THWN Presents: New Voices in Horror 2004 Cyber-pulp Press

"Snake Charmer" originally published in Peep Show 2004

"Park Life" originally published in Shadowed Realms 2005

Copyright © 2007, Doorways Publications and Shaun Jeffrey

Cover design and Interior pieces copyright © 2007, Zach McCain
Voyeurs of Death edited by JG Faherty
Interior Layout by Keith Gouveia

Printed and Bound in the USA
ISBN 978-0-6151-4567-9

For Deb and Callum.

CONTENTS

The Flibbertigibbet

"What's that noise?" Ethan Silverman asked, cocking his head in an attempt to trace the sound.

"That be the Flibbertigibbet, laddie," the old man said, puffing on his pipe, his deep blue eyes narrowed in consternation as he wrestled to land the small fishing boat at the quayside.

"The what?" Ethan frowned and surveyed the rugged mountains surrounding the remote Scottish village of Nocktully on the island of Inchcullen. The next moment he leaned his head back over the side of the wildly rocking boat, fighting the urge to be sick.

"The Flibbertigibbet." The old man shook his head. "Ave ye ne'er heard the sayin'? 'Come ben the hoose and lock yer door, when ye hear the Flibbertigibbet on the moor.'" He winked and laughed.

Ethan shook his head. He was sure the old man was only trying to scare him. "It sounds a bit like bagpipes," Ethan said.

"Aye, it's pipes, but not bagpipes yer can hear."

Realising that he wasn't going to get a straight answer out of the old man, Ethan closed his eyes. He was feeling queasy and he was sure his face must look as green as the sea. The captain, on the other hand, relished the choppy seas. With white hair and beard, he resembled Captain Birdseye, his craggy face testament to the harsh climate.

The water frothed and foamed around the bow like a rabid beast. Seagulls hovered overhead, a choir of noisy angels. Along the coast of the island, the waves battered the rocks into submission and Ethan was grateful when a figure hidden underneath a sou'wester and a thick, black oilskin jacket appeared on the small dock and helped moor the boat, dragging the ropes over the mooring posts with a vicious looking hooked pole.

Shouldering his bag, Ethan staggered off the boat. It took him a while to get his land legs back and he took a couple of deep breaths. He could smell the salty tang of the sea and the fragrant purple heather that clung precariously to the mountainsides. But there was another smell, something unwholesome that the other aromas failed to mask.

He noticed the figure that had helped moor the boat disappearing into one of the small crofters cottages that huddled beneath the grey sky, their roofs slick with rain. The sound of the mournful pipes he had heard from the boat suddenly stopped, and Ethan thought he saw a figure on one of the mountains. Narrowing his eyes, he realised that it was just a stag, its antlers like bolts of black lightning against the dramatic backdrop.

"It were nice meeting yer, laddie," the old man said, chuckling as he scurried toward the nearest house and disappeared inside; the sound of a bolt locking the door was ominously loud. When Ethan turned back to look at the mountain, the stag had disappeared, too.

"Silly old bugger," Ethan whispered. Secretly he was beginning to wonder whether he should have taken this new job. He had only been with the company for two weeks, but it felt a lot longer. If it weren't for the promise of rapid promotion, he never would have signed the contract. He was supposed to be trying to obtain permission for a local leisure facility – a getaway from the strain of modern life, a place where you could do as much or as little as you wanted.

The management stressed that all new employees had to do their bit for the good of the business, and having been divorced for nearly two years, Ethan had nothing else in his life, so he didn't mind coming out to this Godforsaken island if it meant a gold star against his name. He was determined to put his heart and soul into his job. The men at the top were all ancient; people like Ethan were the new blood.

If the facility was built, it would boast a whole host of activities to keep the punters happy: tennis courts, swimming pool, sauna, Jacuzzi, gymnasium, shooting, fishing, archery, beauty salon, quad bikes, orienteering, rock climbing, paint ball. The main selling point would be its idyllic location; away from the hustle and bustle. 'Paradise is closer than you think' was going to be the slogan in the brochures.

Walking along what pretended to be a road, but which was really a rut in the earth that had been compacted by thousands of feet over the millennium, Ethan headed toward what passed as the village pub and guest house. Despite the island's isolated location, the houses all looked neat and tidy with double glazed windows and neatly planted gardens. Ethan knew the neighbouring islands had not fared so well, the islanders having departed for the mainland, but for some reason, the island of Inchcullen seemed to be flourishing.

A sign swung outside the pub: *The Hanging Man*. It depicted a figure with its entrails hanging out suspended by one leg from the branch of a dead tree. Ethan ducked his head to avoid the low doorframe, and entered the building.

Inside, he was surprised to find the bar richly furnished. Plush purple carpet belied the fact that drink and cigarette ash would soon adorn it, and the tables and chairs all appeared shiny and new. Harsh light above the optics seemed to illuminate the bottles contents with an unnatural hue – the rum looked more like blood.

A middle aged man sat smoking a cigarette in the corner of the room. He was staring out of the small window at the mountains. As Ethan approached, the man turned and exhaled a grey cloud of smoke that swirled and eddied as if it was alive. He smiled, his thin lips almost as narrow as his eyes, whose colour was indiscernible below the overhanging buttresses of his eyebrows.

"Ye made it then," he said, grinning salaciously.

Ethan nodded and dropped his bag to the floor, rubbing his shoulder to relieve the strain. "Yes. You must be Duncan Stewart."

Duncan nodded, the movement almost imperceptible. "Yer friends told me ye were comin'." He puffed on his cigarette.

"You mean Janet and Trevor. Are they here?"

Duncan shook his head and gestured out of the window. "They're up yonder mountain. I were beginning to worry that yer wanna goin' to make it." He grinned, all teeth and wild red hair.

Ethan frowned. He felt the man's concern was overly zealous.

Before he could question Duncan further, the mournful sound of the pipes started up again. The sound sent a chill down Ethan's back and he peered out of the dirty window.

Duncan shook his head. "Well, Jimmy, yer here now."

"My name's Ethan, and-"

"Whatever ye say, Jimmy, whatever ye say."

Irritated by the proprietor's manner, Ethan asked, "Can I have the key to my room?" Normally he would have said please, but in this instance, he didn't think his host was genial enough to warrant it. Despite knowing he had to win the locals over, he was damned if he was going to kowtow to everyone.

Duncan stubbed his cigarette out. "There aren't any keys tae the rooms here. Yer at the top of the stairs, first door on the left." He pointed toward the back of the bar and then struck a match down the wall; the phosphorous glare made his face look skeletal and he lit another cigarette and turned to look back out of the window.

Picking up his bag, Ethan walked through the door indicated and climbed the steep stairs to his room. Although he wasn't especially tall, he found that he had to duck slightly. The whole place made him feel rather claustrophobic; being in Nocktully was like being in Toytown.

His room was richly furnished, with a large four-poster bed, a dressing table, and an en-suite bathroom. Like the rest of the island, it was not at all what Ethan had expected.

The sound of the pipes drifted into the room, haunting and eerie. As he listened, he thought it sounded like someone screaming in pain. With a shiver, he drew the curtains in an attempt to drown out the noise.

He decided to unpack while he waited for Janet and Trevor.

***

The mountains around Nocktully were steep and precarious. Purple heather stretched to the foot of the mountains, there replaced by scree and towering buttresses. Janet Clark and Trevor Smyth sat on a large, flat rock and admired the sweeping vista. Far below, the sea frothed and foamed around the island.

"I'll say one thing," Trevor said, "it's certainly beautiful up here."

10

"A bit too remote though, don't you think?" Janet said, running a hand through her damp, long black hair.

Trevor shrugged. "After the hustle and bustle of the city, I think our prospective vacationers will love it." He picked something out of his white teeth and flicked it away.

Fastening her yellow Gortex coat against the elements, Janet hugged herself to keep warm. Personally, she wouldn't pay good money to come to a place like this, not when for the same amount she could relax on a tropical beach.

But it was her job to sell the place; to make sure that the people intending to come to Nocktully were going to have a good time, so she was going to do her best to find things to write a good report about. Her new job depended on it. Although she didn't know Trevor very well, she knew he had a position of authority within the company, so she had to prove herself to him and show willing.

Cupping his hands, Trevor blew into them. "Damn, it's cold though," he said.

"In the brochure the cold will translate into 'a brisk air guaranteed to rid the lungs of the smell of the city'."

"You'd make a good estate agent."

"No one's perfect." They both laughed, but the mirth was cut short as a haunting wail drifted down from the summit of the mountain.

Janet felt as if the sound penetrated her bones and she shivered, her brown eyes wide and alert as she surveyed the rocks.

Trevor stood up and peered toward the summit. "There it is again. Do you think someone's in trouble?"

She shook her head. They had heard the haunting cry twice already today, once from the boat on the journey to the island, and then about half and hour ago, and although she didn't voice it, she felt afraid. There was something unnatural about the sound.

"Do you want to see what's making it then?" Trevor asked, looking toward the summit of the mountain.

Janet almost choked. She coughed to clear her throat. "I don't think so."

"Where's your spirit of adventure?"

"I like my adventures a little tamer, thank you. And if you think I'm going to give you a piggyback when you fall and sprain your ankle-"

"You're not scared, are you?"

Before Janet could reply, a spattering of stones tumbled from the summit. Janet watched them skitter over the rocks and come to rest near her feet and her heart did a quick summersault. They weren't stones at all – they were bones, tiny skulls that might have been mice or voles.

"Jesus," she squealed, tucking her legs up and wrapping her arms around them protectively.

Trevor crouched down and picked up one of the skulls. It was about the size of his thumb, and as white as snow. "It's only a bone," he said, holding it out for Janet to see.

Janet shook her head. "Thank you, but I don't want it near me." She looked up at the summit, about a hundred feet away. "Where the hell did they come from?"

"Perhaps there's an eyrie up there."

"A what?"

"You know, an eagles nest. Perhaps the mother was doing a bit of house clearing."

Although it was a good explanation, Janet wasn't convinced. "Let's get out of here," she said, jumping down from the rock.

"Not yet," Trevor said, shaking his head. "This is perfect. Just think. If there is an eagle's nest up there, the tourists would love it. Let's climb up and have a look."

"*Climb up?* I'm not Spiderman. Have you seen how steep that rock is?"

"Piece of cake."

"Well, I'm not going up there."

Trevor grinned. "Just wait here then, I won't be long."

As Trevor walked away, Janet exhaled a nervous sigh. She watched him clamber over the scree, his red coat making him easy to spot until he disappeared into a gap between two large boulders. She hoped he didn't hold her lack of enthusiasm against her. She needed to keep this job. With unemployment at an all-time high, she knew there were hundreds of people willing to take her place. As she nervously waited for him to reappear, rain started to fall, splattering the rocks like drops of lead and she had to shield her eyes with the flat of her hand to stop the rain stinging her.

Where the hell was he?

As the rain fell, the wind picked up. It tugged at her coat, whipping the lapels across her cheeks.

Ominous clouds were gathering overhead and although it was only midday, darkness descended. Left on her own, Janet's heart beat faster. She could feel the blood pumping through her veins. Something moved near the summit and she saw a dark figure scamper between the rocks. Her breath hitched in her throat. A nervous twitch made her left eyelid flutter. That tropical beach was looking more enticing by the minute. Small rocks skittered down the mountain, but she was too afraid to look at them in case it was more bones cast by a fanciful shaman.

She kept her eyes trained on the mountain, looking for the telltale red coat that Trevor was wearing. She considered shouting for him, but fear had glued her mouth – the consequences of not receiving a reply were too terrifying to contemplate. What if something had happened to him? She was being stupid, but she couldn't help it. Fear conjured fervent thoughts.

Calm down, she thought. Breathe. Nice deep breaths.

Where was he?

As if in response to her thought, she saw a flash of red coming toward her through the darkness and she relaxed slightly. But then she realised that the red glimmer she had seen wasn't scrambling down the rocks – it was flying through the air. She let out a little squeal and stumbled back as the object landed with a splat on the rock where she had been sitting. At first she thought it was Trevor's coat. But it wasn't. Purple steaming entrails slopped over the rocks.

Janet screamed, but the mournful wail of the pipes drowned out her cries.

***

Ethan cocked his head and listened. He was sure he had heard a woman scream before the ominous pipes drowned the sound out.

He looked at his watch. It was three-thirty. Where were Janet and Trevor? They knew he would be here by now. He had sent word that he had missed the train and that they would have to travel to the island without him, and that he would be with them a couple of hours later, so he expected them to be here by now; they had a lot of work to do.

As he walked down to the bar, the mournful tune died away. Duncan still sat by the window, the scene it framed now blurred by rain.

"Have my associates come back yet?" Ethan asked.

Duncan puffed on his cigarette and then turned to face Ethan. "Did ye hear that, Jimmy? That wus the sound of the Flibbertigibbet celebratin'."

"Look, I asked a reasonable question, and I expect a reasonable reply."

Duncan snorted loudly. "Ye damn fool Sassenach."

Ethan could feel himself growing angry and he took a deep breath. He had begun to hate the generic Jimmy title ascribed to him; being called a Sassenach seemed even worse. He found it a bit demeaning. "If you've got something to say, then-"

The door crashed open with a resounding crack and a playful wind entered the bar and tussled Ethan's hair. Then Janet stumbled through the door, her face ashen.

Ethan reached her in two strides and caught her before she collapsed. "Good God. Janet, what's happened? Janet, can you hear me?"

She looked as if she had aged twenty years in the couple of days since he had last seen her, and he noticed grey streaks in her hair that he was sure weren't there before. How old was she, thirty-three? He remembered thinking how attractive she was when they were introduced, but now she looked haggard. Sitting her on a chair, he looked across at Duncan who hadn't moved.

"Get her a drink," he ordered. "Brandy."

Duncan shook his head and laughed as he walked toward the bar where he poured a small glass of brandy from a bottle.

Ignoring him, Ethan turned back to Janet. He stroked her cheek. She was freezing and her lips were blue. "Where's Trevor? Janet, can you hear me?"

"Flibbertigibbet," she mumbled.

"What, say that again," Ethan said.

"It got him."

"What got him?" Ethan frowned.

"Flibbertigibbet."

She wasn't making any sense.

Duncan placed the tumbler of brandy on the table and returned to his seat in the corner, reminding Ethan of a sentry.

Janet downed the drink in one and then sat shivering.

Whirling on Duncan, Ethan said, "What the *hell's* going on here?"

"The Flibbertigibbet."

"Bullshit. This Flibber-whatever doesn't exist. What have you people done with Trevor?"

Duncan laughed without humour. "The Flibbertigibbet must be hungry."

"Listen to him," Janet whispered, her eyes wide with terror. "We've got to get away from here."

"I'll not be chased away by superstitious nonsense and lies."

Janet grabbed his arm and squeezed with surprising strength, making Ethan wince. "We've got to go. *Now.*"

Duncan grinned, revealing a mouth of misshapen teeth "Partial tae a bit of Sassenach it is." He laughed, the sound falling as flat as the joke.

Ethan felt like punching Duncan, but he had never hit anyone in his life. Whatever was going on here, he was going to leave them to it. He knew the company would want their pound of flesh, but he would inform them that the island of Inchcullen was not appropriate for their plans. He would find somewhere else himself for their leisure facility if he had to, but he was damned if it was going to be here.

Without even bothering going upstairs to fetch his bag, he helped Janet to her feet and led the way down to the small dock. Despite the cry of the wind, he could hear the mournful tune. It sounded closer than when he

14

had heard it before and he kept nervously glancing around. The atmosphere was depressing, and shackled by the gloomy clouds, the island was in darkness. There weren't even any streetlights to illuminate the path, and on more than one occasion, he tripped. His heart was racing. He could feel his temples pounding with unease. It was all he could do to stop himself from running. He imagined Duncan laughing to himself and he felt a twinge of anger.

"Where's Trevor?" he asked as they walked.

"He's dead," Janet wailed.

Ethan shook his head. "He can't be dead. They're just trying to scare us." He didn't want to leave an important member of the company on the island because that wouldn't go down well with the management at all. "Where did you last see him?"

Janet pointed at the mountains. "Up there … somewhere."

"Great," Ethan said, realising that Trevor could be anywhere.

The small boat that had transported him to the island was still moored at the dock. It rose and fell in the swell and he could hear wood creaking. Tyres suspended over the sides of the boat cushioned it from the dock.

Hurrying to the house Captain Birdseye had entered, he banged on the door.

"Who is it?" a muffled voice inquired.

"It's Ethan Silverman – you brought me to the island earlier."

"What ye want?"

"I need taking back to the mainland."

Captain Birdseye laughed. "So ye aint deid yet then."

"Of course I'm not dead, you stupid idiot." He couldn't help but get angry.

"It wunna be long now," the captain said, his voice growing fainter as he retreated from the door.

Ethan pounded against the wood until his fists were sore, but he realised it was useless. Captain Birdseye wasn't going to answer.

Well, sod him, sod them all. He looked at the boat bobbing in the waves. "Come on, Janet. If he won't take us, I will."

Janet hesitated. "Can you sail?"

"I can drive a car. It must be similar. Besides, would you rather we stay here with the madmen?"

Janet emphatically shook her head.

"Well, come on then."

Large waves buffeted the quayside, salt spray stinging Ethan's eyes and blurring his vision. The sound of the mournful pipes was closer still. He could hear the tone above the roar of the wind and waves and he looked around, frantic to trace the source when he saw a figure in red hurtling toward them.

Janet screamed, and Ethan almost followed suit.

"Hold on," the approaching figure shouted. "Wait."

"It's Trevor," Janet said, her voice revealing her shock.

As Trevor approached, he had the hood of his red jacket up against the elements.

"I thought ... I thought you were dead," Janet said, shaking her head in disbelief.

"Silly woman," Trevor said, pulling his hood back. "That was just a sheep. The Flibbertigibbet doesn't just feed on company employees you know, and as you wouldn't accompany me it had to eat something."

Ethan wasn't sure he had heard right. He frowned and a sickly feeling gurgled in his stomach.

"Hold on a minute-"

"No, Ethan, it's you that has to hold on." He turned and looked back the way he had come. "Ah, here he comes. Frightful things, these pagan Gods. Think they have all the time in the world."

Ethan peered through the salt spray at an approaching figure and the sick feeling rose to his throat.

Dressed in a kilt of flesh adorned with a sporran of skulls, the Flibbertigibbet sauntered toward them. It had large horns sticking out of its head like a stag and its features were thin and drawn, its eyes glowing white. A shawl of flesh and fur was draped across it shoulder and it carried a set of pipes made from skin and bone underneath its arm. As it pumped the grisly sack, it blew into one of the bones to create the horrendous, mournful tune.

"Why?" he stammered, staring at Trevor. He couldn't believe what he was hearing or seeing and his legs went weak.

"To get ahead in business, you have to have an edge, an advantage over your competitors. This is ours; we've revived a pagan God, and in return for the odd sacrifice, he makes sure our company succeeds."

Janet screamed and backed away.

"Don't worry my dear," Trevor said. "I'm sure it won't be too painful. Just think of it as helping the company."

"Fuck the company," Ethan snarled.

Without hesitating, he ducked his head and charged Trevor like a bull, hearing a satisfying grunt as he struck his foe's stomach.

Winded by the blow, Trevor staggered back and the sound of the hideous pipes suddenly stopped. The Flibbertigibbet took the bone mouthpiece out of its mouth and bared its sharp teeth. It snarled.

"Fuck you too," Ethan snarled back. Although terrified, he wasn't going to die on this shitty little island so that a corporation could make more money from their unholy pact with the devil.

Spying the long pole the man had used leaning against the wall, Ethan grabbed it. The wooden shaft slipped in his hands, and he tightened his grip as he turned to face the Flibbertigibbet.

"If you want me, come and get me," he growled, levelling the point of the pole at the demonic form.

The Flibbertigibbet opened its mouth wide, tilted its head back and laughed. Ethan was shocked. The monster's reaction frightened him more than if it had growled or charged.

"You pathetic piece of shit," Trevor spat, standing upright and rubbing his stomach. "You'll pay for that."

"*Fuck you,*" Ethan roared, pointing the end of the shaft at Trevor and hurtling toward him.

Trevor's expression metamorphosed into a look of fear. He attempted to move aside, but he was too slow. Ethan rammed the shaft into Trevor's stomach. There was a slight resistance as the point of the shaft smashed through Trevor's ribs, but after that, it was unimpeded and he forced Trevor back, putting all of his strength behind the thrust. Trevor gargled, blood spluttering from his mouth.

"If you're hungry, how about a human kebab," Ethan said, pushing Trevor toward the Flibbertigibbet and letting go of the pole.

Without waiting around to see what the Flibbertigibbet did next, he grabbed Janet's hand and forced her onto the boat. Quickly removing the ropes from the moorings, he jumped aboard, almost slipping on the deck as he ran to the cabin. Luckily, the key was still in the ignition and he turned it, the engine spluttering into life. Pushing the throttle, the boat lurched forward, colliding with the dock. High waves battered the side of the boat, and using all his strength, he turned the helm, steering the vessel out into the harsh sea.

Wave after wave battered the boat and Ethan struggled to hold the vessel on a straight course. Salt spray obscured the cabin window and he flicked a switch, hoping that it would operate the wiper, but instead it cast a beam of light like a net across the tempestuous waves.

Before he had time to try another switch, he heard a scream. Janet. His heartbeat went into overdrive and he tried to peer through the spray-soaked window. Large waves crashed over the bow, trying to submerge the boat and he wrestled to keep the vessel heading away from Inchcullen.

"Janet, are you OK?" Ethan shouted. As another wave slapped the vessel, he almost lost his footing. He felt sick. His stomach was doing cartwheels.

Something smacked the window, cracking the glass and Ethan jumped. Illuminated by the searchlight on the cabin, the sea looked red like bubbling lava, and it took him a moment to realise that the window was covered with blood. He opened his mouth, wanted to scream, but he couldn't because he knew that if he started, he would never stop.

Something smacked the glass at his side and he glanced across, horrified to see what was left of Janet's face, the skin ripped from her skull and now stuck to the glass like a macabre stamp. Empty sockets in the flesh showed where her eyes had been, now gory windows on the hostile sea.

Ethan couldn't understand what was happening. And then above the roar of the waves, he heard the pipes. The Flibbertigibbet was on board the boat, playing its mournful tune on the gruesome bagpipes.

The company was going to get its pound of flesh after all.

The Watchers

It was Geraldine's idea.

That's what Luke told himself as he drove through Kidsgrove on the way to Bathpool Park. He had driven to the park before during the day, but at night everything was different, and he almost missed the sharp right turn into the car-park.

The Citroen Saxo's headlights chased shadows through the surrounding trees, and for the first time, Luke felt a little nervous.

He parked the car, and the rumble of a train passing through the tunnel at the edge of the park made the ground vibrate.

"There are some here already," Geraldine said.

Luke looked at the cars dotted around the car-park and nodded. He felt apprehensive and he licked his lips.

"Turn the headlights off. We don't want them getting mad at us."

Despite his nervousness, Luke switched the car's engine off and killed the lights. The illuminated dash went out and darkness flooded the vehicle. He took a deep breath as if about to drown.

From what he had seen in the beam of the lights, there were all manner of cars.

Although unable to see Geraldine, he could smell her next to him. She'd doused herself in perfume, and its cloying scent filled the car. She was dressed provocatively, and he knew she wasn't wearing any underwear as she'd teasingly flashed her breasts and ass before they left the house. He never would have imagined that a chance remark about an activity his colleagues joked about at work would lead them here.

He heard Geraldine breathing at his side, her breaths short and sharp.

Something grabbed Luke's thigh, and he jumped.

"It's only me," Geraldine said. She giggled.

"I know." He wished she didn't speak so loud.

"Well, don't be so nervous."

"Are the doors locked?" he whispered.

"You know they are. You've checked them three times."

Luke nodded.

His eyes slowly adjusted to the lack of light, and he could see the tall trees that formed the perimeter, their branches swaying in the slight breeze.

When he had jokingly talked to Geraldine about Dogging, an activity involving exhibitionism in car-parks that his mates at work had been chatting about, he had been surprised by her interest. It was that interest that had led them here tonight.

He supposed it took all sorts. Everyone found their thrills somewhere. The internet was full of weird practices – when searching

Google for Dogging sites for tonight, he'd discovered it was only one of many strange activities that advertised meetings for people to attend.

Luke wasn't sure whether he wanted to have sex while people (probably perverts) watched. On the other hand, he had never seen Geraldine so turned on. Her excitement was contagious.

He felt her guide his hand between her legs, surprised to find her already moist.

"So what do we do?" she asked breathlessly.

Luke coughed to clear his throat. Despite his trepidation, his penis had gone hard. "We flash our lights or leave the interior light on as a signal to invite people to come and watch."

"Well, what are we waiting for?" She leaned across the seat and found his lips. Her tongue wormed its way into his mouth, as moist as the spot between her legs.

Breaking the kiss, Luke said, "Let's just wait a bit. These might not be Doggers."

"Of course they are. Who else comes to car-parks in the middle of the night?"

Luke didn't like to think. He already knew about the area's infamous history after the Black Panther left Lesley Whittle's body hanging from a wire at the bottom of a drain shaft nearly thirty years ago.

Who knew what sort of people the area attracted.

"You read it on the internet; this is a popular Dogging spot."

"Let's just wait a bit. There's no rush."

He heard Geraldine sigh. She had never displayed this side of her character before, at least not with Luke, and although he didn't like to admit it, it scared him a little.

It also excited him.

Although it was still dark, he could see the swell of her breasts above the neckline of her plunging top. In the near dark the pale orbs could be mistaken for the crowns of two skulls.

Luke shivered at the image.

What's wrong with me? he wondered. Here I am, about to get down and dirty with her. Who cares if someone wants to watch?

But he did care. The thought of other people seeing his girlfriend naked made him feel jealous. Sure other boyfriends had seen her naked (he worked with one of them), but that was before he came along. Now she was his. He often saw men staring at her, admiring her long legs, blondee hair and delicate features with those pouting 'insert cock here' lips, but he could live with that.

But letting people see her naked …

The wind rustled the leaves. In the dark they sounded like scuttling insects. He thought it strange the way sounds were perceived at night.

Luke ran a hand across his brow. He peered outside. "Can you see anyone?"

"Not really. But I bet we would if we flashed the lights."

She was trying to goad him, but he sure as hell wasn't going to let her. He imagined leering faces pressed against the glass. Countless strangers peering in at them like zoo exhibits.

Geraldine ran her hand across Luke's crotch and he bit his lip. Her fingers teased his zip down and eased his cock out. He was powerless to resist. Next minute her head was in his lap, and he could feel her lips sliding up and down his member.

God, she was good. His cock throbbed in need of release.

Something suddenly hit the car and skittered across the roof. Geraldine jumped, and she bit Luke's penis. It wasn't enough to draw blood, but enough to make Luke wince.

She sat up quickly and wiped her mouth. "Sorry babe. What was that?"

Luke peered through the windscreen. He thought he saw movement by the trees, but it was too dark to see clearly. He considered putting the lights on, but was worried that it would be taken as a signal for all the Doggers to come and watch – he wasn't ready for that.

"I don't know. Probably something falling from one of the trees. A stick or a rotten branch … something like that." At least that's what he hoped it was.

He peered at the other cars. Tried to see if he could see anyone in them, but in the dark he couldn't tell. Sometimes he thought he saw someone move, but it could have been his eyes playing tricks.

At least he had locked the doors. That made him feel more at ease, the car his little fortress.

If there was a moon tonight, it was shrouded by clouds and the trees that arched overhead, giving the car-park an almost churchlike aspect.

"How long are we going to sit here?" Geraldine asked.

Not for much longer if you keep whining, he thought. Jeez, she's not usually this impatient.

They had only been going out for a couple of months, but he thought he was starting to know her. Thought they had a special bond. Now he wasn't so sure. There was obviously a lot about her that he didn't know.

"Are you in a mood because you saw me talking to Brian the other day?" she asked.

Luke bit his lip. He had never liked Brian. Now he came to think of it, it was Brian that had started talking about Dogging while they were on a break in the work canteen. Geraldine had been going out with Brian for quite a while before they suddenly split up. Luke thought it served him right

22

to lose such a fox, and then when she had hit on him in a bar one night, he was only too glad to reciprocate.

"Of course I'm not," he lied.

"Well I hope not. He was only asking me for some of his things back that I've still got."

"What things?"

"Oh, you know, CDs, that sort of thing."

Luke drummed his fingers on the steering wheel. "I didn't know you had any of his stuff."

"Don't go funny about it, baby. It's all gone now."

Movement caught his eye and he turned to look through the side window as a match flared, illuminating a face in a phosphorous blaze. The flame didn't stay lit long enough to make out any features, and all he could see now was the glowing tip of a cigarette hovering in a car about forty feet away.

He felt Geraldine's fingers massaging his neck.

Damn, it felt good.

"Baby, I want you," she purred in his ear.

Luke's heart beat fast.

But he still wasn't sure. It didn't feel right.

A car flashed its lights, the sudden glare almost blinding.

When the lights went off, the illumination left a retinal scar. Luke rubbed his eyes.

And then he saw them. People appeared as if out of nowhere. Car doors opened and closed with a funereal thud. Like a procession of shadows, the watchers gathered around the car that had flashed its lights.

Luke heard a click and turned to see Geraldine exiting the car.

"Wait, where are you going?"

She leaned back in, and even in the gloom he had a clear view down her cleavage. "Well if you're not up for it, I'm going to watch."

The door swung shut and he watched her walk away.

"Shit." He zipped himself up and followed. He couldn't let her go out there by herself. Who knew what manner of perverts turned up to watch these things.

As he approached the car, he counted at least eight people crowded around. In the dark it was hard to make out any features, but one thing was certain: he couldn't spot Geraldine.

His heart did a little summersault. Suppose something had happened to her? He would never forgive himself.

The way the crowd stood so still and silent made him feel anxious. He wanted to call out to Geraldine, but was too afraid to alert the group to his presence. In silence he was invisible. The night his cloak.

Creaking tree branches squealed overhead.

Somewhere in the night an owl hooted.

Luke walked toward the car. The gravel underfoot crunched. Luke winced; he tried to ease his feet down to make less noise.

The air smelled of heather and damp earth.

Where was Geraldine?

Luke squinted to see better, but he couldn't spot her.

Close to the car, another noise broke the silence. Deep grunts and rapid sighs.

Despite his nervousness, Luke found the sounds turned him on. He felt his heart pounding in his chest.

When he got closer, the crowd parted slightly and Luke edged between them, eager to see what was happening.

The car door was open, and a figure was kneeling with their head inside the car, bare buttocks exposed to the air.

Luke saw a flash of bobbing long blondee hair.

He recognised it straight away.

Geraldine.

"What the-"

A hand grabbed his arm before he could finish the sentence.

Luke struggled, but another hand grabbed his other arm.

"Let me go you sick fucks," he screamed.

Geraldine stopped her ministrations and turned to look up at Luke. She grinned, her teeth almost luminescent in the gloom.

Luke felt sick.

Geraldine stood up. She'd discarded her few clothes. Luke couldn't believe it. He saw shadowed faces peering at her; felt sick and jealous.

"Geraldine, what the hell's going on?"

Movement behind her and the figure she had been giving the blowjob to stood up.

Even in the near dark, Luke recognised him.

"Brian ... I don't understand."

Brian grinned but didn't speak. His silence was unnerving.

Luke saw Geraldine's breasts wobble as she leaned back into the car. When she stood back up she had a knife in her hand.

The crowd seemed to let out an excited breath.

It was a joke. It had to be a joke.

As Geraldine straddled him, he thought it must be something the lads at work had concocted.

"Look, you can have her back. I don't want her," he squealed, thinking this was perhaps some way to get back at him for going out with Geraldine.

The rustling leaves no longer sounded like insects, but like a scattering of applause. The watchers crowded in, faceless shadows in the gloom of the night.

Brian put his hand on Geraldine's shoulder. "Do it," he said.

Luke realised that he'd been duped in an elaborate setup.

These people weren't here to watch people have sex. They were here for something far more gruesome. He remembered the sites on the internet. Strange sites offering stranger practices. Bestiality. Defecation. Snuff movies. Satanic rituals.

A cornucopia of depravities.

He watched the knife descend, a shooting star of forged steel - wished upon it that whatever practice they indulged, they wouldn't prolong the pain.

Paranoid

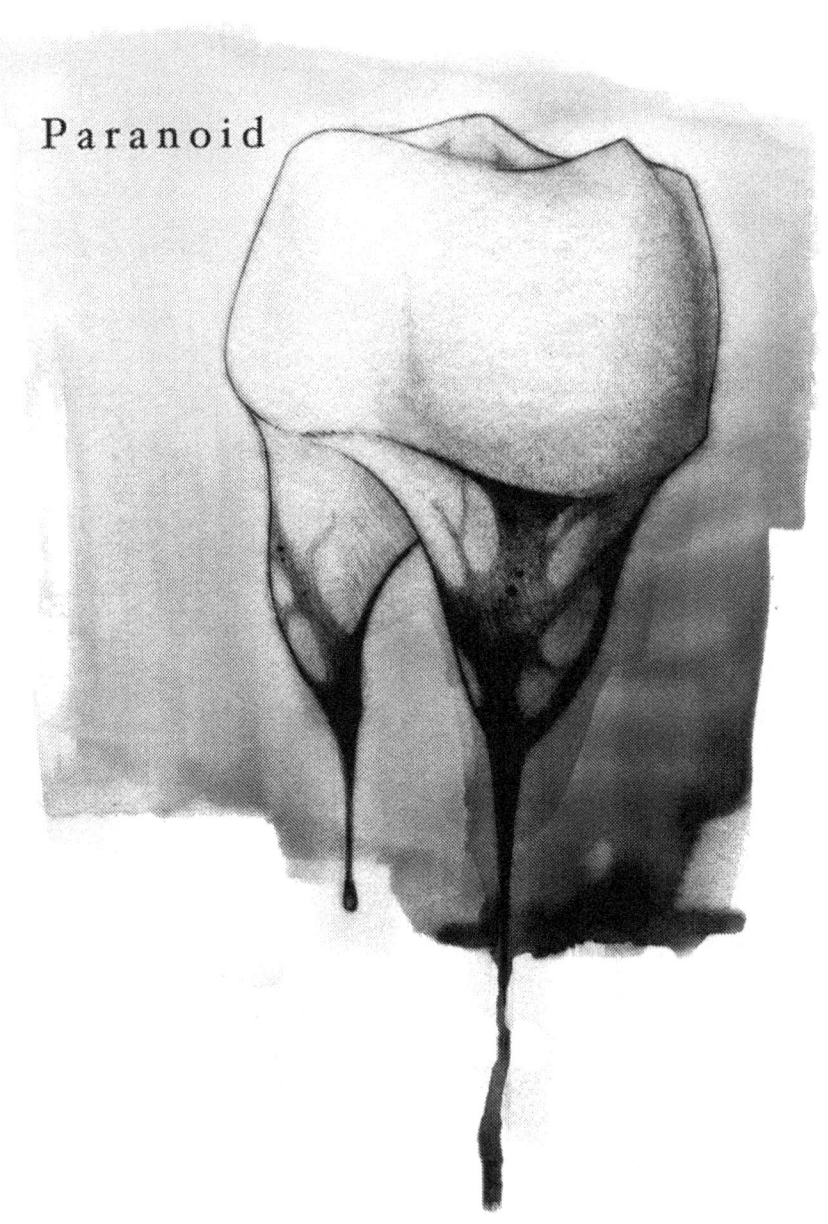

Where am I?

The woman sat up in bed, the disturbing enquiry immediately followed by another, much more chilling question.

Who am I?

A sharp pain shot through her head, as though someone had driven a lance through her brain. She cringed and cradled her face in her hands, waiting for the pain to subside.

When she felt able to move her trembling hands away, she looked around, barely controlling the panic that threatened to overwhelm her.

Beams of sunlight streamed through a long window, the Venetian blind angled to throw morbid prison-bar shadows across the floor. A series of unlit fluorescent lights dotted the tiled ceiling. Several beds similar to her own, some of them occupied, were arranged in the room. An antiseptic smell permeated the air. It slowly dawned on her that she must be in a hospital.

But how did I get here? And why am I here? What's happened?

Her heart began to beat even faster. She cautiously pulled down the bed sheet to inspect her body, fearful she might discover missing limbs or organs. She sighed with relief when she saw both legs extending from a blue gown that seemed much too small for her plump body. She pulled it up over her bosom, but everything seemed to be in order, no scars or bandages.

She clenched her fists. Pursed her lips as she tried to recall anything that might help. *Damn it, why can't I remember?*

"Hello," she called to the patient lying opposite her.

The grey-haired woman didn't reply. Didn't even acknowledge that she'd heard.

"Hello, can you tell me where I am please?"

The woman remained oblivious to her.

She looked from one bed to another. All the occupants appeared comatose, their eyes lying in pockets of shadow, mouths set in petulant frowns. Were they drugged? Was this a funny farm? She hoped not, because if it was, there had been a mistake. She wasn't mad. She couldn't be, could she ...?

Her initial fear was slowly being replaced with a physical and mental fatigue. She shook her head to hold off the growing lassitude. As she did so, she noticed a call button hanging from the headboard. It had a glowing orange button with a picture of a bell, so she pressed it. Almost immediately a ringing noise sounded somewhere outside the room.

A moment later, she heard heavy footsteps approaching and the double doors at the end of the room swung open. A nurse walked in. As she marched through the beams of sunlight streaming through the windows she appeared almost angelic, a halo of light framing her face which wore concern like a mask.

"Where am I? What am I doing here?"

The nurse reached out and took the woman's wrist, timing the thunderous pulse against a pocket watch on her apron.

"You're alright," she said, her voice conveying years of bedside manner, "You …um, had an accident. Don't worry if you can't remember. To tell you the truth, it's sometimes better not to."

An accident! What sort of accident? Where were the bruises?

The nurse slipped a thermometer between the woman's lips as she was about to ask more questions. The woman gazed at the nurse's dazzlingly white teeth, noticed a cavity in her Upper Right Lateral. She didn't know how she knew the term, thought it an odd thing to know. Something about teeth tried to rouse a memory, but it wouldn't surface.

"Just hold it under your tongue. That's it," the nurse said. She took a small torch from her pocket and shone it in the woman's eyes, making them water. Then she walked to the foot of the bed and inspected a chart. A moment later, she returned to take the thermometer out. "The doctor will be around later to check up on you. Try and rest for now."

With that, the nurse walked away, leaving the woman even more puzzled than before.

She sat back. Why aren't I covered in bruises? Not sure she had looked properly last time, she lifted her gown again to inspect herself more closely. But there was nothing. About to pull the gown back down, she noticed what might have been a series of small puncture marks in the crook of her left elbow. She gingerly touched the marks, wincing when she found them to be tender. Someone had injected her.

Then again, perhaps I'm a drug addict. How the hell was she supposed to know anything when she couldn't remember.

It was strange - no, *terrifying* - not remembering anything about herself. Was she married? Did she have a partner? Children? There were so many questions. How old am I? Do I have a job? Beyond the here and now, a thick, black veil barred every avenue of thought.

A white butterfly fluttered through an open window and alighted on the bedside lamp. It flapped its wings once, twice. Something about them…their movement, gentle and graceful, was familiar. She fought to bring the recollection into focus, but it disappeared into the grey mist shrouding her memories. In a sudden burst of anger, she grabbed the creature and crushed it between her fingers.

Then she closed her eyes, allowing the thick, black veil to descend, and she welcomed the void.

***

When she next awoke, the lights were on and a man stood over her. She jumped, her mind a jumble of thoughts until she remembered she was in a hospital. She assumed he must be the doctor, but he didn't look much like one. Too young, his face too angular, almost as though it had been chiselled from a block of ice; he radiated no warmth for her well-being and his eyes were as black as night. Across the other side of the room, the nurse administered an injection to the feeble artery of a sickly grey haired old woman.

"How do you feel?" the man asked gruffly.

"I've got a headache," she said, noticing the onset of gingivitis around his gums.

"I'm not surprised." He turned around and consulted her chart. He scratched his chin. Then he walked away and spoke to the nurse, and although they were too far away for her to decipher the conversation, they both seemed to look at her as though she were a specimen under a microscope. For a moment, she had a vision of the doctor standing over her holding an array of surgical implements and a bloody mask covering his mouth. The thought made her shiver.

"So what kind of accident did I have?"

The doctor turned and stared at her. The nurse whispered something in his ear, and then he said, "Don't worry. Everything's fine now."

"But what was it? What happened?"

The doctor shrugged. "I'm not at liberty to say."

It was like talking to a damn machine. Realising she wasn't going to unearth the truth, she decided to let it lie for a while. One way or another, she'd find out soon enough.

Before she left, the nurse put an extra pillow behind the woman's head and helped her sit up. Of the eight beds in the room, five were occupied. Her fellow patients seemed taciturn, and when she tried to engage them in conversation, they were unresponsive.

Every so often, the nurse entered the room and drew a screen around one of the patients, shielding proceedings and adding a secretive aspect to the place. She began to find the Venetian blinds troubling. Wasn't a hospital supposed to be a bright environment for the patients' well-being? She couldn't understand why they didn't open them fully to let more light in.

The old woman in the bed directly opposite sat looking at a television - unfortunately, it wasn't switched on.

Unable to see much from her bed, she slid her legs out and stood up. For a second she felt dizzy. *How long have I been lying here?* When she felt steady, she approached the window and lifted the corner of the blind. She was surprised to see bars on the window.

She turned around, confused. One of the beds was shrouded by a screen and elongated shadows scratched at its surface. Assuming there must be a nurse in attendance, she approached the screen and pulled it aside to ask about the bars, but there was no one there. Startled, she shook her head and hurried to the woman in the next bed.

"Excuse me; I was wondering if you could tell me what hospital this is?"

The woman looked up and her lips cracked. She cackled loudly and then looked back at the blank television screen.

It was damned disconcerting. This wasn't right.

She wanted to shout at the woman, shake her, anything to get a remark from her, but she didn't. What was the point?

Goosebumps mottled her arms and she shivered. The bumps looked like complex Braille. She wondered whether they held her secret within their complexity.

One thought came clearly to mind: *I need to get out of here.*

The floor was sticky beneath her bare feet as she walked toward the doors. She dared not guess what sort of contaminated leftovers she was walking in. When she reached the doors she pushed, but to her surprise, she found them locked. She knocked, banged and shouted, but no one came. What the hell was going on?

The doors had little circular windows in them. She peered out, but the corridor beyond was dark and she couldn't see anything. She stepped back, noticed her reflection in the glass and gasped. They had shaved her head and there was a circular scar around her crown. She gingerly touched the scar, tracing its path around her head. *What have they done to me?*

Suddenly feeling sick, she returned to her bed and pressed the call button repeatedly, but still no one came. She leaned down to check the chart at the end of the bed, but it only had a listing of her basic patient information, pulse, temperature, weight, etc.

On the line marked name it simply read: Jane Doe.

The place felt like a prison. If it was a hospital, this was not a regular ward.

The old woman opposite grinned at her as though privy to a secret.

Perhaps she was being paranoid, but everything seemed too ethereal.

What have they done to my head?

***

It must have been nearly an hour before the door opened and a stocky young man walked in, pushing a trolley laden with drugs. He had short brown hair and a nervous tick in his left eye; round glasses lent him a studious air. He pushed his spectacles up onto the bridge of his nose and walked down the ward, making notes in a folder.

When he reached her bed, the woman pretended to be asleep. After he walked past, she quietly unplugged the bedside lamp, picked it up, tiptoed across the room and smashed it over his head.

The lamp broke and the man collapsed to the floor. The woman opposite clapped delightedly. Without hesitating, she stripped the man and put on his clothes. A quick search of the pockets revealed a surgical cap that she pulled carefully over her tender scalp. She also found some loose change and a pen. His shoes were too big for her, but she wasn't going to complain. Without waiting to see if he was going to get back up, she ran for the door, the loose change jangling in her pocket. Luckily, he'd left the door unlocked.

At the end of the corridor direction signs marked out paths; each direction colour-coordinated with lines painted on the floor.

She followed a blue line that led to the exit.

When she came to the reception area, she ducked her head and made her way through the waiting patients.

She was almost to the door when she noticed a little freckle-faced, blondee-haired girl holding a bloodied handkerchief to her mouth. A woman sat comforting her. They looked like mother and daughter.

"Doctor, can you just take a look at my daughter? We've been here ages and no seems to be taking any notice," the woman said.

It took her a moment to realise the girl's mother was talking to her. She looked around to make sure no one was watching.

She considered ignoring her, but thinking that might attract attention if the mother made a fuss, she said, "What seems to be the problem?"

"It's my daughter; I think she's swallowed her tooth. She fell over, you see."

She knelt down and asked the little girl to open her mouth. Straight away, she noticed a missing Upper Right 2nd Bicuspid.

Everything seemed to suddenly fall into place – memories flooded back. "Well if you want to wait here, I'll take your little girl through and see what I can do."

The girl's mum nodded her head. She looked relieved.

The woman took the little girl's hand. It felt warm in hers. The nurse and doctor that had attended to her earlier were standing next to a drinks vending machine, talking. Head down, she led the girl past and into the hallway. Then she followed the red line along the floor.

"Can you really find my tooth?" the girl asked.

"Of course. And when I do, there'll be a shiny coin for you. How's that sound?"

The girl smiled.

***

"How's that new patient responding to the drugs?" the nurse asked.

The doctor sipped his drink. "Only time will tell. I sometimes think if these cases weren't so tragic, they'd be funny."

The nurse nodded. "Just thinking about it makes me cringe. It makes you wonder what some people are capable of. Heaven knows how she got in that little boy's bedroom. If his mother hadn't come along and knocked her out ..."

The doctor sighed. "Last week I had my third case of someone who thought he was Napoleon, but this is the first time I've operated on someone who thought they were the Tooth Fairy." His expression turned suddenly pensive. "Those growths on her back were the oddest thing though. Some sort of deformity, not unlike a hunchback I should say. Perhaps they're at the root of her psychosis."

"Has anyone been able to find out who she is yet?"

"Not that I know of. I'm sure someone will come forward and put a name to her eventually." He gave the nurse a crooked smile and tapped his left cheek. "Pity she's not who she says she is though; I've got a molar that's been killing me." He laughed.

The nurse shook her head. "I think you're confusing her with a dentist. Tooth fairies only take teeth that have fallen out."

"Well they're in the wrong line of business. Have you seen how much dentists charge? They should branch out."

"Excuse me, Doctor."

He looked over to see a young woman standing there. She held a bloody cloth in her hand.

"Yes?"

"I was wondering if you could tell me where the other doctor took my daughter?"

"Other doctor?"

"Yes, the heavyset woman. My daughter lost a tooth in an accident. The doctor said she'd take care of her. They went that way," the woman added, pointing down the corridor.

At the end was a sign with an arrow: Surgery.

"There aren't any women doctors on duty today," the nurse said.

33

"Oh, god." The doctor dropped his cup and raced down the hall, the nurse close behind him. When they reached the surgical ward, he flung open the doors and then stopped.

The body of a young, blondee-haired girl lay on the operating table. Entrails slopped from the open cavity in her chest to lie coiled on the floor. Blood still dripped off the edges of the table. A scalpel lay alongside the corpse; beside it rested a pound coin speckled with blood. The doctor picked up the coin.

The nurse stumbled out of the room, holding her stomach and retching.

In the sudden quiet, he heard faint laughter and what he recognised as the musical jangle of coins. Returning to the hallway, he looked around but saw no one except the nurse, who stood bent over a rubbish bin.

Another sound reached his ears. Light footsteps running.

Or perhaps the beating of oversized wings.

The Tunnel

I can still remember the look on his face...

It had been almost twenty years to the day since I last saw my childhood playground where I used to scurry about in the tall fields of grass with my friends, our paths as delineated as rabbit runs. Now the grass didn't seem anywhere near as high or imposing; as if I had eaten Alice's fabled cake, the world had become a smaller place.

Standing at the edge of the road, I looked to my right. The trees we used to climb were gone, pulled down to make way for a housing estate. I sighed and shook my head, depressed by urban infringement. All those summers when the days seemed to last forever had been spent around here, climbing trees, jumping brooks, making dens. This was where I had my roots, where my fondest memories had been spawned...

And where my nightmares originated.

Even though the sun was shining, my shoulders shook with an unpalatable chill. A lot of my memories of youth are now blurred, lacking in detail, but the memory of that day twenty odd years ago returns to me again and again with unnerving clarity ...

***

"Come on, Runt," I shouted as my young brother Aaron fell behind, his head visible above the grass as he tried to locate us. My friends had run on ahead, and I was torn between waiting for Aaron and leaving him behind. I knew he would find us if I left him, but I felt responsible for him, and so I waited, giving an exaggerated sigh of impatience when he eventually caught up. His cherubic little face was flushed.

"Sorry," he said as he tried to catch his breath.

I shook my head and ruffled his mop of unruly, sandy-coloured hair before crouching down on the ground.

"Jump on then," I said with mock irritation, unable to hold back the smile that was bursting to come out. As he settled onto my shoulders, I stood up, surprised by how heavy he had become. "Jeez, Runt, at this rate you'll be carrying me soon."

Aaron laughed, and the sound captured the essence of that summer.

He dug his heels into my sides. "Come on then, Bruv, gee up," he joked.

I made a neighing sound and Aaron clucked his tongue to urge me on. Following the tall hedgerow, I galloped toward the large horse-chestnut tree in the far corner of the field.

The sky was vivid blue, the sun a golden crown fit for a king. Being a loyal subject, I paid homage by going topless to bask in its radiance. Sweat trickled down my back, ran down my sides like an army of ants.

The tree grew on the edge of a small wood. It was by far the tallest tree in the world and I could see Danny waving at us from within the tapestry of leaves. I smirked, secretly proud of the fact that I was the only member of our gang who dared climb to the utmost branches, from where I swear you could see the whole world on a clear day.

Even though there were other trees easier to climb, we never ventured into the wood itself. It was silly really, but we were scared of the old Victorian house that stood in the middle of the wood; in the winter, you could see it through the skeletal branches. Although it was hidden by foliage in the summer, it made its presence felt in the shadows. The trees were also home to rooks that circled the house like cackling witches, an early warning alarm that sounded when anyone ventured too close to the house.

The old horse chestnut's trunk had a spine of six-inch nails that we had hammered in with a rock a couple of years ago to help us climb the difficult trunk. As we reached the foot of the tree, Danny dropped out of the higher foliage, followed by Rachel. Although she was a girl (a fact which had become more obvious of late), she could climb almost as high as me. Tim appeared next, followed by Justin and Paul. The gang, dropping like conkers.

"What kept you?" Danny asked.

I dropped Aaron to the ground, gave a counterfeit disgruntled sigh, and tapped Aaron on the head. "The Runt couldn't keep up."

Aaron looked up at me and frowned, which made me feel slightly vexed at having to make excuses for him all the time.

"Come on then, we're going over the fields," Rachel said, swatting a fly away from her face.

I was painfully aware of how she had begun to affect me, and I was disappointed that I wouldn't have the opportunity to sit in the highest branches, the perfect vantage point to surreptitiously peer down her top.

"But we've only just got here," I said, still exhausted after giving Aaron the piggyback ride.

Tim adjusted his glasses and shrugged. "It's not our fault you took so long."

As if that was explanation enough, they started to walk away, following the barbed-wire fence that imprisoned the wood, its subtle terror restrained within a flimsy barrier.

I looked at Aaron as he scrawled his name on the tree trunk with the chalk I had bought him for his birthday.

The path my friends took ran beneath an archway of trees that looked like a huge, green wave. I followed them, ignoring my brother's plaintive cries as he tried to keep up.

I clambered over the gate and then crunched over the gravel driveway leading to the old house, its dark windows and ivy encrusted walls momentarily visible. Although I tried not to look at the building, movement in one of the windows caught my eye. It was only a fleeting glance, but I thought I saw something flutter behind the glass, leaving me with the retinal imprint of grinning skeletal features. Or perhaps it was just my impression of the sun's reflection.

I shivered and turned to look back along the tunnel of trees. Aaron was chasing a cabbage white butterfly at the edge of the tall grass and I silently urged him to catch us up. I would have at shouted him, but I was too unsettled by my closeness to the house. After all, anyone could be listening.

Looking back at the house, I shivered and then vaulted the gate on the other side of the drive and started to cross the field, anxious to put a bit of distance between it and myself. As the house was old and eerie, one would assume there would be stories about it, a rich history of ghosts, hangings, murders, illicit affairs and such that had been passed down through generations, but there weren't. It was as if the house had so intimidated the town that people were afraid to even create rumours about it.

Ahead of me, Paul clambered over a fallen tree trunk that had lain untouched for as long as I can remember, its surface blanched so that it resembled a large tusk, a relic from some prehistoric beast.

Rachel had already reached the stile that spanned the brook, and she was excitedly waving at us to catch her up. Anxious to please, I overtook the others in my haste. Thudding onto the stile, I smiled shyly at Rachel and looked where she pointed.

"Look at that," she gushed, her pigtails drooping over her cheeks as she leaned forward, her bosom squashed against the stile post.

I looked down and saw the object of her excitement: a sheep's carcass. Its body had dammed the brook, creating a small reservoir that lapped gently over its woolly coat, trickling like tears over its head.

"That smells disgusting," I said as the others caught us up.

"Anyone bring the mint sauce?" Justin asked as he clambered down the bank to get a closer look.

"That's gross," Rachel shouted after him.

Tim sat on the stile and pulled a pack of cigarettes from his pocket. Striking a match on the wooden post, he lit a cigarette and blew a cloud of smoke into the air, his lips pursed in a kiss to an imaginary succubus.

"Anyone want one?" he asked.

"Nah," I said.

When Rachel accepted one, I quickly changed my mind. I didn't know whether it would impress her, but she always seemed to talk to Tim more than anyone else. Accepting the cigarette, I put it in my mouth, not quite sure what to do with it.

"Just suck hard until you're in," Tim said as he offered me a light.

My resultant coughing fit made everyone laugh.

"You'll get used to it," Rachel said, showing me how it was done and then flicking ash into the brook.

"Yeah, just do like Rachel and pretend it's a dick," Justin shouted up.

Rachel selected a large rock and then threw it into the reservoir, splashing Justin with water as he inspected the carcass.

"Bloody hell, that water's filthy. I might catch something."

"A cold if we're lucky," Rachel agreed, nodding her head.

I glanced at the source of the stream, a pipe that disappeared into the bank in the direction of the old house. None of us had ever had the nerve to find out where it went. The hole was large enough to enter if you stooped. Not that any of us would. I could only see a few feet along the pipe but that was far enough to assure me I wouldn't want to enter it. There could be rats or anything in there. I also suffered from claustrophobia; when in a confined space, I felt as though someone was squeezing the air from my lungs.

"How long have you been smoking?"

I turned at the sound of Aaron's voice and blushed at being caught with a cigarette in my hand.

Predicting my fears, he said, "Don't worry, I won't tell mum or dad."

I gave him a playful punch on the shoulder. "Thanks, Runt. I owe ya."

He smiled up at me.

"Go on then, Runt," Danny ordered. "Run along that tunnel and tell us where it leads." He bent down and peered along the pipe.

"No way," Aaron squealed.

Rooks circled overhead, cackling.

Tim blew a ghost of smoke at Aaron's face. "Yeah, go on Runt. You're the smallest. It'll be easier for you."

"On me own? Not a chance."

As Aaron backed away, the rest of the gang closed ranks and hemmed him in. I leaned against the stile; the cigarette had made me feel ill.

"Tell 'em," Aaron implored, looking up at me. "Tell 'em to leave me alone. I don't want to go in the tunnel."

The gang turned to face me and I sensed the unity between them. I licked my lips and looked at my brother. He looked scared.

Too weak to defy my friends, I shrugged my shoulders. "Don't worry, Aaron." It was the first time I had used his name in years. "You'll be

OK. Just go and have a little look." I silently begged him to comply, otherwise I could see the others manhandling him into the tunnel, and that would really scare him. "If you get lost, just wait and I'll come and find you."

That seemed to reassure Aaron; he looked up to me in many ways, and as he wiped a tear from his eye and stepped into the tunnel, the expression on his face was one of forced determination. He offered a wan smile, and then he turned and disappeared.

I never saw my brother again.

The police failed to find any trace of Aaron, and after the search was abandoned, a metal grille was placed over the tunnel entrance. My parents held me responsible (I think their subsequent separation was also blamed on me), and the guilt weighed heavy on my shoulders.

After the incident, I lost touch with my friends, but I don't remember exactly when or how that happened. It was as if they had also disappeared in that tunnel. The only one I remember with any semblance of clarity was Rachel. I eventually lost my virginity to her, entering another dark and mysterious tunnel; after our brief encounter she disappeared as well.

It seemed as though everyone I cared for had become a memory; insubstantial, just fleeting glimpses of subjective reality. Sometimes I wonder if they ever really existed.

It's taken me twenty years to face my fears. Twenty years haunted by nightmares. Fear and guilt are terrible burdens to carry for such a long time, and I am now a shadow of my former self.

Crossing the gravel drive, I looked toward the old house. The years had failed to diminish its haunting presence, but to me, it was now just a house.

Continuing on, I reached the stile and looked down at the gaping mouth of the tunnel. I noticed the metal grille had corroded and fallen away, a rusty web lying on the bank. Perhaps stories of the house had finally started circulating, providing adequate deterrent, which is why no one bothered replacing the cover.

I took a deep breath to calm myself, and then I jumped down into the water and waded toward the dark entrance.

The rooks roosting in the trees suddenly took flight, cackling as they circled the house, announcing my unseen presence.

Twenty years ago I had been too afraid to enter the tunnel – I was no longer afraid, and my brother had waited long enough.

With one last look at the sky, I ducked and crawled into the tunnel. It was a tight fit, my grown-up body squashed into the pipe. I cringed at the slimy appearance of the walls, which glistened like an artery, making me wrinkle my nose.

My childhood claustrophobia had long vanished, and I crawled on unperturbed. The water trickled through my hands and legs, like sand through an hourglass.

Sounds permeated the tunnel; I stopped to listen.

"Aaron," I whispered, the sound of my voice magnified in the tunnel. No one answered.

Continuing on, I followed various tunnels and peered down each tributary until I heard what sounded like a child, crying.

The sound made the hairs on my head prickle and I cocked my head and listened.

There it was again, a faint, choking cry.

It seemed that the noise originated from another tunnel to my right, and I headed along it, calling Aaron's name.

Up ahead, I noticed movement and I increased my speed until finally, in the dim light, I spied a crouched figure.

"Aaron," I said, choking back ephemeral tears.

The figure quivered.

"Aaron, I've come to find you."

The figure shivered and slowly turned. My heart stopped and tears filled my eyes. He looked just as I'd remembered him

His sandy-coloured hair was wet and stuck to his cheeks, just as it was when he died. I could tell by his red-rimmed eyes that he had been crying.

Running a hand beneath his nose, Aaron said, "I got lost."

I fought back tears of my own at the thought of him down here for all those years.

"I waited for you, just like you said, but you didn't come, did you?"

His accusation hurt me.

"I'm here now," I replied, gathering him in my arms.

When I finally released my grip, I took him by the hand and led him out of the tunnel, into the light.

If it had not been for my own untimely death in the car crash yesterday, I would never have been able to find him.

Now together, we would rest in peace.

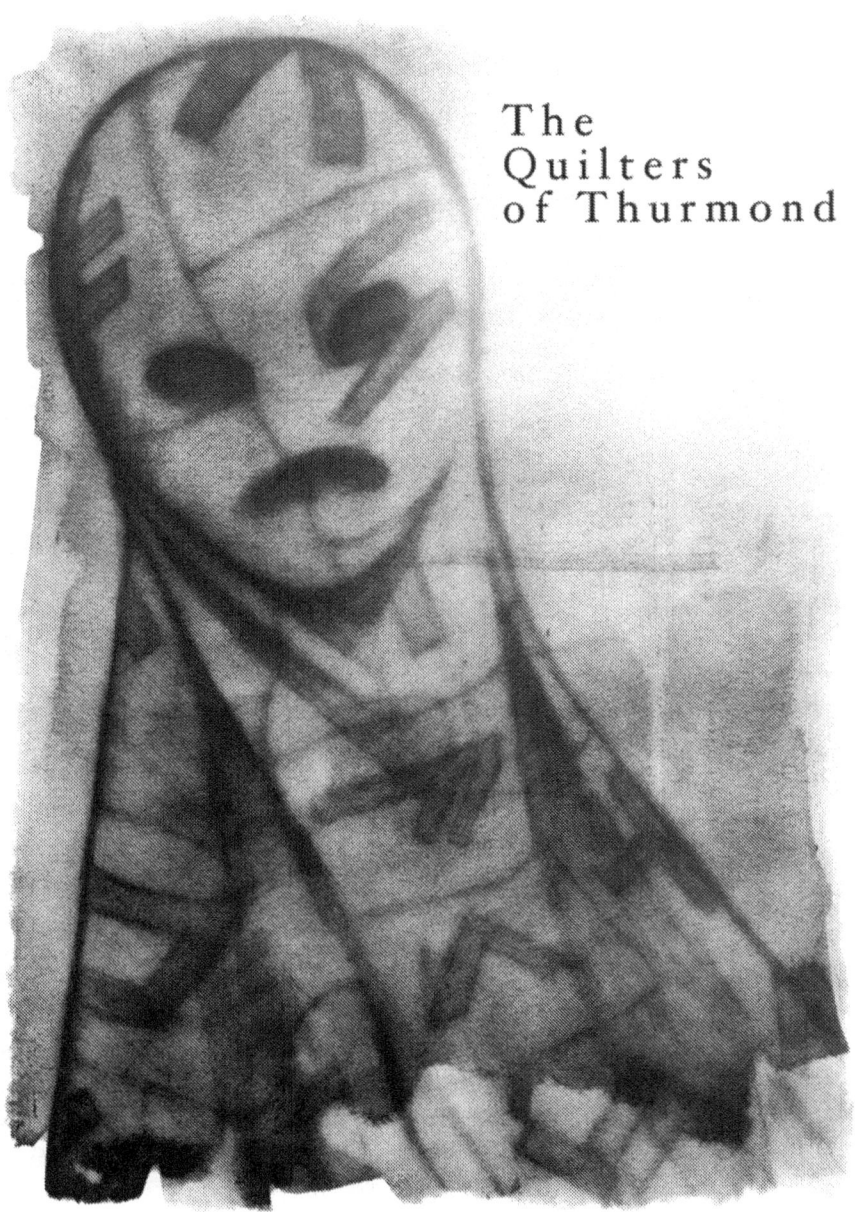

The
Quilters
of Thurmond

The needles pierced the quilt with a precision honed through years of practice, weaving together pieces of material to form a multi-coloured tapestry.

Jean Harvey admired her portion of the quilt, nodding with smug satisfaction.

"This is gonna be a good one," Helen Jones said as she took a length of thread between her teeth and snapped it in half.

Jean basked in the approving nods from the quilters that sat around the bedcover. It gave her a warm feeling knowing that they were here at her request as she had been for them. Naturally her daughter, Amanda, wouldn't appreciate all of the effort that had gone into the quilt's construction. She called the women's get-togethers a waste of time, always joking that the women's guild was into recycling before anyone else had ever even heard of it.

Jean ran a hand through her grey head of hair before selecting another piece of fabric. Many of the pieces stitched into the quilt contained Celtic symbols and other decorative motifs, the meanings of which would be lost on her daughter who didn't concern herself with the old ways.

The bedcovers used to be made as wedding gifts, but times had changed and most of the young girls nowadays seemed unconcerned with marriage, preferring to live out of wedlock. To move with the times, and to keep the tradition alive, the ladies of Thurmond now made a quilt when one of their daughters' was leaving home instead, and their fingers bore the brunt of how busy they had been of late.

The advent of television seemed to be to blame. It had revealed a big wide world beyond the insular island. As a result the youngsters showed no interest in the island's history or its traditions. Before television, the closest Thurmond had come to entering the Twentieth Century was when old Jack Hutchinson purchased an automobile, not even considering the fact that the island had no suitable roads. The vehicle now resided in one of his fields, little more than an expensive chicken coop.

When the quilt was finally finished, Jean looked at it with a sense of satisfaction. The bedcover was large enough to hide a double bed beneath its borders. But naturally Amanda would protest about taking it with her, they all did, saying that they could purchase one on the mainland instead of having to carry the extra weight.

"Now it's time for the binding," Jean said. She picked up her needle and stared at the quilt, admiring the almost invisible stitches that held it together. Placing the point of the needle against the whorls of her thumb, she pressed it into the callused flesh and drew blood, letting tiny drops fall onto the fabric. The other quilters did the same, the drops of blood soaking into the design, invisible to the naked eye. Outside, a cockerel crowed and the sun was obscured by thick black clouds that rolled in from the sea. The first drops of rain pattered against the window, drowning out the soft chant that issued from Jean's mouth.

**

Amanda gave her mother what she considered to be her most disapproving glare. "You must be joking," she said. "I'm not taking that mangy piece of cloth with me to London. What would people think?"

Jean shook her head. "You young uns today. Now, when I was a girl-"

"Yes, I know," Amanda said. "We don't know how lucky we are. All you had to play with was a clothes peg dolly with a painted face. I've heard it all before. Now get off my back. I'm not taking it, and that's final."

She watched her mother stirring the broth on the hob; didn't like the way she smiled as though privy to a secret.

"I mean it mum, I'm not taking it." She crossed her arms below her chest, pushing up her ample bosom.

"If you say so dear."

"What, is that it; no lecture or anything?"

"If you say you're not taking it, then that's fine."

Amanda pursed her lips. She didn't like the smug expression on her mother's face. Didn't like it one bit.

**

The fishing boats were just returning with their hauls when Amanda and her parents reached the harbour. Nets were strung up over mooring posts as though a gargantuan spider had spun a web during the night. Seagulls hovered in the air and sat perched on the quay as they waited for the fish to be unloaded.

Tiny houses bordered the harbour. Smoke drifted from their chimneys like umbilical cords to unite them with the sky.

"I'll be thinking of you," Jean murmured into her daughter's ear as the captain of the small boat impatiently blew his horn and pointed at the watch on his wrist. "Now you run along and don't forget to write. I want to know everything you get up to. And remember, don't you get mixing with any of them men on the mainland. They're only after one thing, especially with an attractive girl like you."

Amanda rolled her eyes to the heavens. "Mother, I think I know how to take care of myself."

She kissed her parents on their cheeks and then clambered onboard the boat while her father hefted her suitcase up after her.

Once the boat set sail, Amanda stood at the stern, watching her parents shrink into the distance. Ironically, she thought the clouds above the island resembled a patchwork quilt and she felt a momentary twinge of guilt at refusing to take the bedspread.

The journey was unremarkable. Apart from Amanda and the captain, there were a couple of crew who went about their business with barely a glance her way.

Once she arrived on the mainland, Amanda knew it was too late to make the journey to London, so she walked toward a guesthouse on the quayside that had a 'vacancies' sign in the window. She found the prospect of leaving home and starting a new life so far away daunting, and she was more than a little afraid, but she couldn't stay on Thurmond. It was dead; most of her friends had already left. Luckily, she had managed to secure a job in the city working in a restaurant through a friend of the family. It wasn't anything special, but she had been promised board and lodging which was probably worth its weight in gold.

Lights had already started to come on around the harbour, their reflections fragmented on the surface of the water. She humped her suitcase up the three steps to the front door of the guesthouse and tried to peer through the net curtains that obscured the glass panels in the door, but she couldn't see anything. She opened the door and a bell chimed, announcing her presence as she walked inside.

A jovial, balding, middle aged man with a paunch appeared in the hallway. He reminded her of the store owner from the Mr. Ben cartoon she used to watch, the man who always popped up at the appropriate time.

"Good evening," he said. "Can I help you?"

"Hi, yes, I noticed you had vacancies, and I wondered if I could have a room for the night."

The man nodded his head. "Certainly. We're not very busy at this time of year, so you can take your pick." He opened a ledger on a small reception desk. "It's £20 a night for bed and breakfast. Is that okay?"

Amanda nodded. After the boat journey, she was keen to rest and would have paid treble that amount.

As she signed the register, the man said, "So what brings you here?"

"I've just arrived from Thurmond. I'm on my way to London."

"London! The bright lights of the big city. I went to London once. Hated it. Too many people."

Amanda smiled. "Well I guess it's not to everyone's taste."

The man shrugged. "I guess not. Would you like a harbour view? There's a room at the front, nicest one in the place."

"Why not."

"Here, let me help you with that suitcase." He grabbed a key from a hook on the wall and stepped around the reception to help her.

The room was on the first floor. After the proprietor let her in and left, she stared out the window at the sea. Thurmond seemed like a distant memory.

As she was only staying for the night, she hefted the suitcase onto the bed and unzipped it to unpack a nightgown and toiletries. She removed the top layer of clothes and placed them on the dresser until she spotted her nightgown. It had a Mickey Mouse motif on it, and when she reached the city, she planned to throw it away and purchase a new, sexier one in case she ever got lucky and brought a boy back. About to close the case, she noticed a flash of brightly coloured cloth. She grabbed the material and tore it out of the case.

The quilt.

Amanda had spent the night packing the case herself, but her mother must have repacked it, taking out some of her clothes to fit the bedcover inside. Her face flushed red with anger and she sucked her top lip as she took a deep breath. How could she! A quick inspection of the remaining clothes in the suitcase revealed that her favourite blouse, a jumper, a number of t-shirts and two pairs of jeans were missing to accommodate the blasted quilt.

She stared at the bedcover and shook her head. Her mother had promised she didn't have to take the bloody thing. The bedcover seemed even more garish in the sombre surrounds of the room, the bright, bold colours almost glowing in the fading light.

After a moment, Amanda threw the quilt on the floor and stormed out of the room and went outside to take deep breaths. It wasn't so much that she was bothered about the clothes. It was the principal of the matter. Her mother had lied.

Outside, the wind buffeted her face, the taste of brine redolent in the air. Boats bobbed in the harbour and ropes clanged against masts like giant wind chimes. Coloured lights from a pub at the end of the harbour spilled across the pavement. In need of a drink, Amanda walked across to the pub and entered.

Nautical décor hung from every available space. Buoys, nets, fishing paraphernalia; it felt like walking into Neptune's lair. Amanda ordered half a lager from the young girl behind the bar and retired to a secluded corner, the floor at her feet mottled by cigarette burns like bullet holes,

A few couples sat huddled around the room, leaving space between themselves as though wrapped in their own private worlds. Amanda turned away to stare out the window. Brightly coloured lights from the pub's front illuminated the sea. Further out, a rising moon looked like an ulcer on the roof of the world.

She took a long gulp of her drink. At least now she was free of Thurmond and its stalwart traditions and medieval ways. When she went back to the guesthouse, she would dispose of the quilt. Let's see how her mother would feel about that when she told her. The thought made her smile.

"Hello. Amanda, wasn't it?"

Amanda looked up to see the guesthouse owner standing beside her.

"I don't mean to intrude if you want to be on your own."

"No, no, please, sit down if you want." The man looked pleasant enough, and she thought talking to him might help take her mind off the blasted quilt and her mother.

"Well, let me buy you a drink. What'll you have?"

She could imagine her mother's indignation if she knew a man from the mainland was offering to buy her a drink, even if he was old enough to be her father. "I'll have half a lager, please," she said.

The man grinned. "My name's Mathew," he said before walking across to the bar.

***

Amanda couldn't remember how many drinks she'd downed, but she was sure it wasn't enough to make her feel how she felt at the moment.

She stared across the harbour, the surrounding lights even more fragmented than before. Everything looked slightly blurred, made her feel dizzy. She felt someone at her side acting as a crutch.

"Don't worry; we'll be home in a minute."

She recognised the voice as that of Mathew, the guesthouse owner. She giggled to herself, felt a sense of euphoria.

Once back at the guesthouse, Mathew helped her up the stairs. He unlocked the door for her, and then led her into the room. She saw the quilt lying on the floor where she had discarded it. She giggled again.

"Here, let me help get you undressed," Mathew said.

Amanda chuckled. Everything felt surreal. "I'm a big girl. I can do it myself."

"I can see you're a big girl," he said, breathing heavily against her ear.

She raised her hands in a 'whatever' expression, her eyes rolling in her head, making the room spin. She felt Mathew's fingers fumbling with the zip on her jacket and she sniggered as he pulled it down.

"That's it, let's get you out of these clothes," he said breathlessly as he slipped her arms out of the sleeves.

Amanda reached down and fumbled with the button on her jeans, giggling again when she couldn't undo it.

Everything looked blurry, made her feel out of kilter. She looked down, saw the quilt on the floor. She tried to focus on it, but it seemed to be moving, the patterned scraps of cloth merging in a whirl of colour.

She felt Mathew pawing at her breasts, but she felt unconnected, as though it wasn't happening to her. She felt his fingers slide along her back, searching for the clasp of her bra.

Mathew snorted. "I've never been very good with these," he said. "It's a good job you're the only guest I've got at the moment, otherwise we might have disturbed someone when we get started. I like to hear girl's scream, you know. The louder the better."

Amanda was hardly listening. She felt compliant, like putty in his hands.

She noticed the quilt moving again and she tried to focus on it. The bright colours seemed to intensify, almost blinding her. She wanted to shield her eyes, but couldn't be bothered.

As though there was something underneath it, the quilt suddenly rose up. Amanda chuckled.

"Cool," she said.

The quilt rose higher and higher, began to take form behind Mathew's back.

"It will be when I get this blasted bra off," Mathew said. He grabbed the straps on either side and pulled, snapping the clasp. "That's better." His hands slid around to fondle her breasts.

Amanda stared at the quilt. Watched as it took shape. Indents appeared. Valleys formed. Areas tightened, moulded into what she recognised as a torso, followed by legs and arms. Finally a head formed from the cloth, sunken areas defining a mouth and eyes, the protuberance of a nose forcing itself out.

The patchwork figure stepped forward, grabbed Mathew from behind and pulled his suckling mouth from her nipple. Taken by surprise, Mathew gasped. He twisted his head to look behind him and emitted a high pitched scream.

"It's a good job there's no one here to hear you," Amanda chuckled.

Mathew rammed his elbow into the quilt, but the material hardly moved under the impact.

She watched him struggle as the quilt engulfed him, circling its arms around his torso. She saw what looked like sharp needles burst out of the cloth and puncture Mathew's skin, but she couldn't be certain. Her vision was deteriorating, becoming blurrier by the minute. Then she blacked out.

***

Amanda woke with a start. She opened her eyes, blinking against the bright sunlight. She was lying on the bed, and she sat up straight, still feeling a little disorientated. Her memory of last night seemed hazy. She rubbed her eyes and yawned. The curtains were open, and she heard the cry of a seagull as it wheeled in the sky outside her window.

She looked down to find her t-shirt bunched above her breasts, the remains of her bra dangling at her sides. A memory tried to force its way through the fog in her mind. She had gone out for a drink. She had been speaking to someone.

With no recollection of how she came to be in the state she was, she tugged her t-shirt down and stood up. She noticed something bright from the corner of her eye and stared down at the quilt. She put her hands to her mouth in shock. There was someone underneath it, their figure perfectly outlined.

Had she brought someone back to the room? She tried to remember. Who the hell was it? Suddenly embarrassed, she backed away.

From a distance, it looked as though someone had pushed the quilt down around the figure to accentuate their contours, almost smothering. Something about the shape seemed familiar, and she suddenly recognised the paunch, the shape: the proprietor, Mathew.

Surely she hadn't … No, she wouldn't. Not with him. Another thought occurred to her. What if he had drugged her? Jesus! She gasped and stumbled back, a sick feeling forming in her stomach.

Suddenly angry, she stepped toward the bedcover and grabbed the corner, but the quilt deflated like a balloon, and as she lifted it, she found there was no one there.

Confused, she let go of the quilt and watched it drift to the floor. She thought she saw the guesthouse owner's face imprinted in the intricate weave, his mouth open in a silent scream bordered by bars of thread.

As the quilt settled, the image dissolved.

Amanda shuddered as a memory returned, that of the proprietor touching her up. Revolted, she tugged off her t-shirt and put on a new bra. Then she quickly pulled on a fresh top and started stuffing her clothes into the case. Once packed, she crouched down and gingerly picked up the quilt. The familiar and yet comforting aroma of her mother emanated from the material. After a moment, she carefully folded the bedcover and placed it on top of her clothes. As she closed the lid, the material rippled as though someone was taking a final breath.

Once packed, Amanda left the guesthouse and headed for the train station. She didn't quite understand what had happened last night, the memory still too hazy to decipher, but she made a mental note to ring her mother when she arrived in London, to say thank you and to acknowledge that perhaps she did need to learn about the old ways.

But for now she had a long journey ahead, one that no longer seemed so frightening.

Sin Eater

The knock on the door froze Frank's blood in his veins. He looked at Lucy, his wife of fifteen years, and saw the same fear mirrored on her prematurely aged face. Married at sixteen, parents by seventeen, neither of them looked their true age. Lucy had wrinkles where there should have been smooth skin, and dark blemishes accentuated the bags beneath her eyes. Frank knew he didn't look much better. The wedding photo hanging above the mantelpiece was so removed from the couple sitting in the armchairs at either side of the living room; it may as well have been of strangers.

Justine looked across, eyes wide, lower lip starting to tremble. "Don't answer it, Dad," she said, a slight tremor in her voice.

Frank glanced at his daughter. His tongue felt like sandpaper as he tried to work up enough moisture to speak.

"Darlin', you know I have to answer it."

Justine flinched. "Please, can't we pretend we're not in? Just this once?"

"It knows we're here. It always knows; just like it knows when to come," Frank replied.

"Daddy ..."

"It's no good, Justine. You know what'll happen if I don't let it in. The same thing that happened to Lily Evans' family ... And the Browns'."

"I don't like it," Tommy said from the floor, clenching a crayon so hard that it snapped in two. The open page of his colouring book had been obliterated by a mass of black and red strokes.

As much as he agreed with his son, Frank knew they were powerless to say no. He set down the model ship he'd been carving and stood slowly, as though he had a dumbbell in each hand. With slumped shoulders and legs barely strong enough to hold him upright, he crossed the room. He could feel the eyes of his family boring into him, could practically taste their fear in the air.

The hallway stretched before him like a long tunnel. The porch light seemed like a distant glow, ineffective against the surreal darkness. He could see the shape of the thing behind the glass outside. Already grown impatient, it bobbed anxiously from side-to-side.

He caught a glimpse of his reflection in the hallway mirror, and mentally berated himself for the timid demeanour it radiated back.

Grow a backbone, you sack of shit, he thought as he straightened himself up.

He reached out to unlock the door. His hand shook and he willed it to stop, to reflect a calm appearance. But it was no good. His fear had taken control, as it always did.

The latch turned in his sweaty fingers and he pulled the door open. A draught of cold air rushed in, bringing the Sin Eater with it.

Frank recoiled from the creature's presence.

Dressed in a long, flowing garment that had seen better days, the Sin Eater moved silently into the house. Face hidden beneath a cowl, it bore an impeccable air and Frank could only trail after it like a man on his way to the guillotine.

In the living room, the Sin Eater sat down in Frank's chair. It placed a hand on each arm, and nodded its head toward Lucy.

She slowly stood and made her way across the room. Frank stayed by the door. He could see that each step Lucy took seemed to sap what little strength she had left. She knelt before the creature and kissed its outstretched hand. Her lips puckered upon contact as though tasting something vile.

Frank rubbed his face. He could see tears forming in the corner of Lucy's eyes. He hated himself for allowing his family to be subjected to this humiliation.

When the Sin Eater spoke, its voice was harsh, commanding.

"Feed me," it boomed.

"Three days ago, I ... I took something that wasn't mine. I ate a couple of loose grapes from the bag before paying for them. I stole," Lucy said.

Frank clenched his fists.

The Sin Eater appeared to grow in size, appeared to almost consume the chair. "Continue. Tell me more."

Lucy visibly trembled. "Two days ago, I ... Frank ..." She looked at her husband. He nodded his head and turned his gaze to the ground. "I lied to my husband. I told him I was going shopping, when really I went to play bingo." She blushed.

Frank pinched the bridge of his nose between thumb and forefinger. "How many times have I told you not to gamble?"

The creature nodded its head as though enjoying watching the family squirm.

"I ... I've also had wicked thoughts. Thoughts involving another man."

"Tell ... me ... more," the Sin Eater said, each word spoken on an inhalation of breath.

"It was our neighbour. Mathew Upton. Forgive me, but I had carnal thoughts about my neighbour." She looked up at Frank and then quickly bowed her head in shame.

"Continue," the Sin Eater commanded. "Tell me what those thoughts were."

"I ... I can't," Lucy stammered.

The Sin Eater visibly rose from the chair.

Frank rushed across the room and knelt by Lucy's side. "It's okay. Tell him."

Lucy twisted her head to look at Frank, tears of shame running down her cheeks.

"I'm sorry, Frank," she whispered.

Frank squeezed her shoulder to offer encouragement.

"I imagined taking him into my bed," Lucy said. "I … I imagined him making love to me. I imagined him … sucking on my breasts."

"Muuum," Justine said, covering her ears.

"That's good," the Sin Eater said as it settled back down in the chair.

Frank looked behind him. Tommy was colouring on a piece of paper with a black crayon, trying to distract himself. His tongue poked from the corner of his mouth as he concentrated on the task. From where he knelt, Frank could see that the picture was of a scratchy demonic face with two white spots left blank where the eyes should be.

He looked up at the Sin Eater. He had never seen its face beneath the cowl. Someone – it might have been Jack Harper – once said that Monica Hutchinson had seen it. However, no one could verify the claim. Not after Monica disappeared. All Frank could see now were shades of darkness mixed on a canvas of bone. He looked quickly away.

Lucy finished feeding the Sin Eater with a couple of minor sins, and then stood and skulked back to her chair.

The Sin Eater nodded toward Justine.

"I'll go next," Frank said, forcing the words past the hard lump that had formed in his throat.

As though sensing Justine had more juicy titbits with which to feed it, the Sin Eater shooed Frank's offer away with a sweep of its arm.

Justine padded across the room like a nervous animal. She looked at her father as if for some way to stop what was coming, but Frank shook his head in defeat.

She's only fourteen! he thought, clenching his fists. She shouldn't have to go through this at her age.

"Feed me," the Sin Eater said.

Justine gulped. "Two days ago, I … I …"

She looked at her family for support, but there wasn't any to give. Lucy had her face hidden in her hands, crying. Tommy continued to colour. Frank tried to give her a comforting smile, but he could feel it morph into a grimace. He ground his teeth and clenched his fists harder, feeling his nails bite into his palms.

Tears streamed down Justine's cheeks. She choked, snorted loudly to clear her nose. "Two days ago, I got drunk with a group of friends and I—"

Enough was enough. His family didn't need this indignity. Enraged and finally empowered, Frank stood up and ripped the Sin Eater's cowl off.

The creature lifted its bald, monstrous bloated head and fixed him with two, beady black eyes. If the eyes really were the mirror to the soul, then Frank thought the Sin Eater contained all the evils of the world. Its flesh looked like pounded meat, giving it an even more grotesque appearance. It parted its lips in a malevolent grimace, revealing crooked, stained, but very human-looking teeth. Some of them appeared to have amalgam fillings.

Around its neck, half-buried in the raw, oozing flesh, was a black clerical collar.

A memory came to Frank: the sudden departure of Father Finnegan from the church after a brief illness.

Father Finnegan, who'd heard confession four nights a week.

Could it be...?

The Sin Eater growled and started to rise, but Frank was faster. He snatched the craft knife he had been using to carve the ship and slashed it across the creature's throat. Skin parted, but instead of blood, a deafening cacophony of multitudinous voices gushed out, unburdened sins that had kept the creature fed. Frank slashed again, and again. He couldn't afford to stop. Not now. When the cries eventually died down, all Frank could hear were the muffled sobs of his family.

***

Frank waited in the silence with only his thoughts for company. It was cold. He shivered, arms folded across his chest as though to lock in the warmth. He hoped he hadn't waited too long. Since the death of the Sin Eater he'd felt like a pressure cooker, his sins building up inside his skull like a good head of steam. He had to rid himself of them before it was too late. Before he started to —

The confessional window suddenly slid open. Frank took a deep breath.

"Forgive me father for I have sinned."

He wondered how long Father McMichael would last.

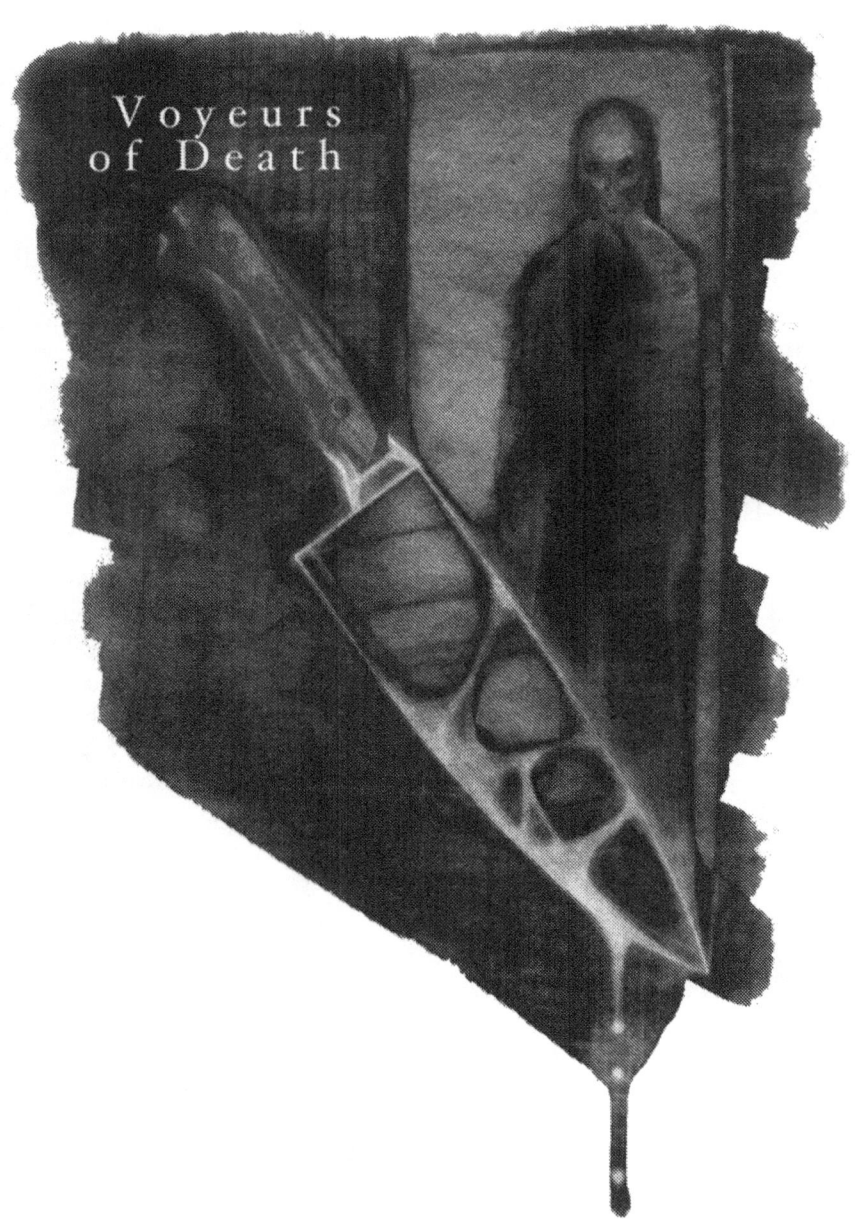

Voyeurs
of Death

The squeal of brakes preceded a grinding crunch of metal as the bonnet of the BMW folded like a concertina. The windscreen exploded, firing shards of glass into the vehicle. Daniel Lane shielded his face, the bright lights of the vehicle into which he had collided the last thing he saw before the airbag inflated, throwing a cloud of dust into the car. Daniel's head flew forward, the airbag smothering as much as cushioning. The seatbelt snatched tight across his chest and he actually thought he felt his brain rattle inside his skull with the force of the collision.

He didn't even have time to see his life flash before his eyes as the world went black.

Time became abstract, and when his awareness slowly returned, he felt strangely buoyant. He opened his eyes to find himself hovering naked in the air above the mangled wreckage of the two cars.

Stunned, terrified, and self-conscious of his nakedness, he moved his hands to cover his penis.

What the blazes is going on?

His body seemed insubstantial; wispy, as though composed of smoke.

He looked down at the cars, saw himself, his physical self, slumped in the driver's seat. The sight stunned him even more, his mind a whirl of emotions and thoughts. Am I dead? he wondered. Although a wind blew, he had no sense of temperature, felt neither hot nor cold.

He thought about going closer to have a better look, to check out the state of his physical body, and as soon as he thought it, his hazy form drifted down toward the wreckage. Everything on the edges of his vision appeared blurred, making him feel dizzy.

Smoke curled from under the crumpled bonnet and water from the broken radiator streamed down the road as though the vehicle was relieving itself.

White dust from the airbag covered the face of his otherself in the car, made it impossible to gauge his condition. Was he breathing? He looked for signs of movement — the twitch of an eye, the flexing of an arm — but his physical body remained perfectly still.

He had no sense of smell. Couldn't hear either. He felt as though he was trapped in a vacuum.

Thank God Mandy wasn't with me, he thought, relieved that his wife had decided to stay at home with a headache rather than accompanying him to the works disco, which had been a fiasco anyway. The office temp Carol had been coming on to him all night. Not that he would have succumbed; he loved his wife too much. But it was an ego boost to know other women still found him attractive.

He glanced at the vehicle into which he had collided (couldn't even recall who had crashed into who); saw a body lying sprawled across the bonnet, legs still trapped inside the vehicle, wedged by the steering wheel. Blood spattered the silver paintwork, dripped over the metal radiator grille. Wanting to get a better look, Daniel only had to think about moving and his ethereal body drifted closer, but as he drew near, he gasped and turned away. The man's face had been sliced by the windscreen as though it were a cheese grater. Grotesque strips of flesh hung from the man's cheeks, and one of his eyeballs had popped, releasing a stream of viscous fluid.

Cars pulled up along the road, the occupants peering at the scene from the safety of their vehicles – voyeurs of death.

A few people exited their cars, started to approach the wreckage. A tall, gangly man with a balding crown walked straight through Daniel's insubstantial form as though he wasn't even there. Daniel noticed the man shiver as he passed through.

Overhead, the moon appeared from behind baleful clouds like an ulcer on the mouth of the world.

Daniel spun around, his mind reeling with thoughts. He stared at his physical body again; thought he saw the slight flare of his nostrils as he breathed.

From somewhere in his memory, he recalled tales of people having near death experiences being able to see themselves from above, what some people called out-of-body experiences. He wondered whether that was what this was.

No longer embarrassed by his naked form, he tried to attract peoples' attention, waved his arms, tried to speak, but it proved useless. No one could see him.

What if he was trapped like this forever? Stuck in limbo. The thought made him panic. Made him grieve that he might never see Mandy again. As soon as he thought about his wife, his ethereal body began to move through the air, faster and faster. The roads below snaked through fields and villages. Despite the speed at which he was travelling, he felt little sense of movement, and for a moment, he marvelled at his ability to fly unaided.

After a while, he recognised the landscape below, the roads familiar, even though he was high above them, and next minute, he found himself on the street where he lived. Most of the large detached houses resided in darkness, but light emanated from his own abode. He sped down toward his house and slipped painlessly through the bedroom window and drifted back toward the door.

The sight that met his eyes left him feeling sick and confused. His loving wife Mandy lay naked on the bed, hands clasped to the handle of the knife protruding from her stomach. Blood flowed between her fingers and soaked into the sheet beneath her, blossoming like a rose around her body. Matted strands of her long blonde hair adhered to her sweat-soaked breasts.

Even in death, she looked beautiful.

Daniel wanted to be sick, but his insubstantial form didn't have the capacity for such a reaction. He stared at his wife, unable to look away.

Movement by the closet caught his eye, and he turned to see a naked young man struggling to pull his trousers up from around his ankles. The man's penis had shrivelled up like a worm as he tussled with his clothes. And all the time, he stared at Daniel, his eyes wide with shock.

Can the son of a bitch see me? Daniel wondered.

He didn't recognise the man, had never seen him before. He watched as he hobbled away, his trousers like shackles. The man's mouth opened and closed. Unable to hear in his present form, Daniel didn't know what the man was saying, but no amount of remorse would ever be enough.

Angered beyond belief by the death of his wife, Daniel was about to rush toward the murderer when he felt a spasm through his body. The next thing he knew, he felt a sharp tug originate around his bellybutton, and then as though yanked by an invisible cord, he was pulled through the walls of the house and back toward his physical body.

He flew at such speed, the landscape blurred, shades of black interspersed by streaks of illumination from streetlights and car headlights.

With a final jolt, he found himself back in his physical body and was immediately struck by pain in his chest, a result of the crash. He gasped, snapped his eyes open and sucked in a deep breath.

Numerous pairs of eyes peered down at him as he lay on the road, obviously dragged out of the car by someone. A woman knelt beside him, her face a mask of concern. She ran the back of her hand across her mouth.

"Thank God," she said. "I thought you'd died there for a minute."

Daniel coughed and struggled to sit up.

"Take it easy," the woman said. "There's an ambulance on the way."

Ambulance! He didn't want an ambulance. Mandy was dead. He wanted revenge. Someone had taken away the love of his life. What good was a bloody ambulance?

Ignoring the woman's pleas, he staggered to his feet. Pain originated from points all over his body, but he ignored their warnings.

A thought clawed its way through the pain. A ray of light in a sea of darkness. What if Mandy wasn't dead? He tried to remember the tales he had heard of out of body experiences. Hadn't he read that when in such a state, time no longer exists, that someone out of body transcends time. If that were true, there was still a chance. Perhaps that's why this happened.

The thought brought fresh hope. Spurred him on. Perhaps he had been granted a glimpse of the future. He staggered around the wreckage, his legs like tubes of flesh devoid of muscle and bone.

The morbid spectators followed close behind, and Daniel turned and spat at them. Not normally uncouth, he didn't have time to explain to them what had happened, or to try to explain that of course he wasn't mad.

He heard the sound of an engine ticking over, traced the sound to a blue Citroen Saxo parked at the side of the road, and hurried across.

He wondered which of the spectators the car belonged to, but wasn't about to ask. He yanked open the door, settled into the driver's seat and pulled the door shut.

Faces pressed against the side windows, their breath misting the glass. Someone banged against the boot. Shouted something unintelligible.

Ignoring the protests, Daniel put the car in gear, released the handbrake, eased off the clutch and pressed the accelerator down as far as it would go. The engine roared and people scattered like tenpin bowls.

He drove like someone possessed, hardly taking his foot off the accelerator as he took corners at breakneck speed.

He didn't know how long it took to reach his house, the journey a blur, but when he arrived, he jumped out of the car and stared up at the bedroom window, hoping to see Mandy.

Unable to see anyone, he staggered up the path, unlocked the door as quietly as he could, and crept into the kitchen. No way was he facing a killer without some from of protection. He grabbed a sharp knife from the draining board, and then headed toward the stairs, hoping and praying that he wasn't too late.

At the top of the landing, he heard a muffled groan originate from their bedroom. The sound chilled him to the core. Mandy! He took hold of the door handle, turned it and barged into the room.

Well prepared to find his wife dead, he wasn't prepared for the sight of a man's naked buttocks as he thrust into Mandy.

On hearing Daniel enter, Mandy peered around the side of the man lying on top of her, unwrapped her legs from around his body, and exhaled loudly. Sweat coated her face; dripped from her forehead.

"Daniel, I thought … you're early," she said breathlessly.

The man lying on top of her rolled aside. It was the man from the vision. He stared at Daniel and shrugged.

"Sorry mate, you know how it is."

Daniel could hardly believe his eyes. He stumbled forward, more sickened to find his wife in bed with another man than if she were dead.

"How could you," he roared.

Mandy reached to pull the sheet across to cover her nakedness. Daniel found the action ironic considering he had seen it all before. In fact, the action made the event seem even tackier than it already was.

"Oh, for heavens sake, Daniel," Mandy said. "Get a grip. We're all adults."

Daniel looked at the knife in his hand. He looked closer;

recognised the handle. Had seen it protruding from Mandy's stomach.

He looked back at his wife, felt a knot tighten in his gut. How could she do this to him? Face contorted in rage, he marched across the room, the blade jutting from his fist like a talon.

The voyeurs of death are going to love this one, he thought as he set the scene.

Life   Cycle

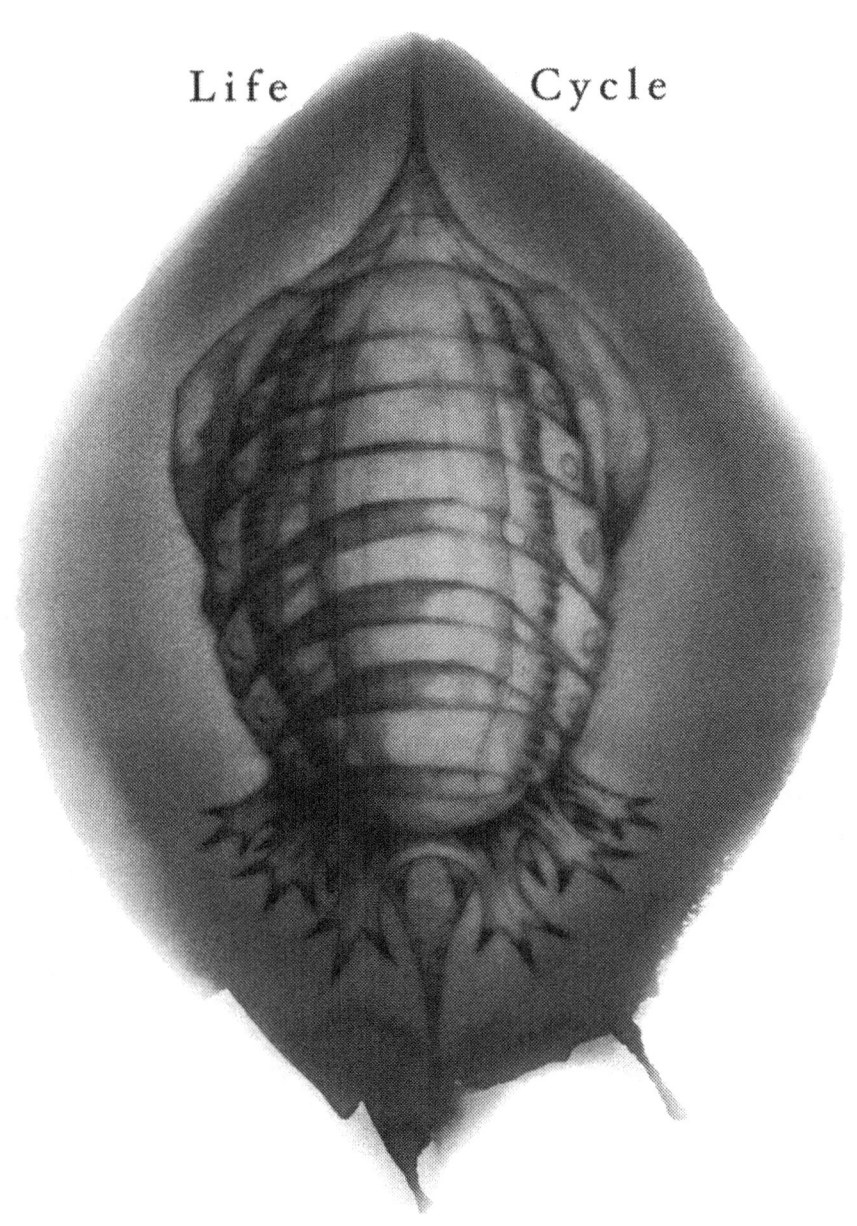

Phase 1

Frances Hulme woke with a start. Pain surged through her body and she clutched her swollen stomach. Sweat beaded on her forehead.

Since it had started to show six months ago, she had tried to deny the baby's existence, but she couldn't deny the pain. She felt it kick, felt it lash out within her womb. Why was this happening to her? A baby was the last thing she wanted.

When it first started to show, she got away with baggy clothes and quick sexual liaisons up dark side streets, but eventually the bump got in the way. Then, her regular customers disappeared in droves. They probably wondered who the father was, and if there wasn't one, they probably worried she might try to pin it on them. Even Frances didn't know who the father was. There had been so many men. Faces were a blur. She always used contraception, but when you got through as many rubbers as she did, it was inevitable that some of them split.

Another spasm shot through her body. She felt sick. She never dreamed the pain would be so bad.

A doctor or abortion clinic had been out of the question. They would have spotted the puncture marks on her arm that were mingled in with the insect bites. Besides, her friend Fiona Jones went to the doctor complaining of a pain in her head. She never came back. That wasn't going to happen to Frances. No way. She had contemplated a back-street butcher, but she had heard stories of it going wrong, and the thought of someone sticking a needle between her legs had put her off. She didn't want her livelihood damaged. Her attempt at pummelling her own stomach and even falling down the stairs hadn't got rid of the thing, but she knew from some other girls on the street that a lot of pregnancies never came to term, so she had just hoped that it would die inside her.

But it was too late for that now. The thing was alive and well and wanting to come out.

The faint orange glow of a streetlight shone through a crack where the curtains didn't meet, which told her that it was about seven o'clock.

When the curtains were open, the light was enough to illuminate the room, and Frances often used it to save her electricity. Now, with the curtains part drawn and the light casting an orange pall, the room looked sickly and cancerous. But it was light enough for her to see the syringe already prepared on the tin foil.

She grabbed the rubber strap that was coiled next to the syringe. With one end in her mouth, she tied it tightly around her upper arm. Next she picked up the syringe and squirted the air out, losing a few precious drops of the amber liquid.

She had never had the urge to prepare her house for the birth, which she believed was referred to as nesting. Instead, she let her mess accumulate. Old newspapers and empty takeaway cartons littered the floor. The smell was horrendous. But the drugs would soon take that away. And they would take away the pain. Without the drugs, she never would have been able to cope these past few months. How people managed without drugs, she never knew. The pain of giving birth was incredible.

She heard something scuttling across the ground, and saw an iridescent blue beetle of some sort foraging among the litter. The bugs seemed to thrive in her damp ground floor bedsit, and no amount of chemicals or sprays could kill them. Some mornings she woke to see slug trails across the ground – if she stared at the trails long enough, she started to see letters forming, but she would wipe them away with her foot, afraid that the invertebrates were trying to communicate with her.

She tapped her arm to bring up a vein. Naked and with the sheet pushed back, she could see the baby moving. Irregular shapes protruded through her taut flesh. From the corner of her eye, she saw another beetle scurry along the skirting board.

When her vein had risen, she punctured it with the needle and squeezed the drug into her body.

It didn't take long for the familiar warm feeling to penetrate her system. She lay back and loosened the rubber strap.

Frances had tried most drugs on the market, but this new one, Paras something or other - she couldn't remember the exact name - was the best she had ever tried. It worked almost immediately. Her regular supplier didn't know where it had come from; just that it was the fastest selling shit they had ever seen. The market was flooded with it.

The drug soon quelled the pain and she felt almost buoyant. In these states she became almost maternal. She wondered if she would be able to recognise the father in the baby's features, and she giggled to herself. She patted her stomach and the baby shifted.

Life was good.

Motherhood might be good too. She could sell the baby. She hadn't thought about it before, but she could make money out of this. And God, she could do with some. With not working these past few months, the meagre bit she had put by had dwindled to almost nothing.

Barren couples would pay good money for her baby. She smiled. Something good could come out of this after all.

Her fingers tingled slightly, and despite her dreamy state, she felt the urge to push. Her money pot wanted to be born.

Frances complied. Knees up in the air, she pushed. Sweat trickled down her face and she gulped breaths. Her shoulder length black hair was sodden and it stuck to her face. Through the drug-induced delirium, she

Voyeurs of Death

vaguely felt the contractions, and she pushed harder. She wondered how much money she would be able to make. Thousands, she supposed. At least enough to offset what she had lost.

Suddenly she felt her waters break, soaking the mattress, but she wasn't bothered. She would have enough money to buy a new mattress when she sold the baby.

Frances guessed that she had been pushing for an hour when her offspring suddenly popped out.

Unable to see clearly from where she was, she sat up, looked down and frowned. Something was wrong. Where there should have been a baby, there was what she could only describe as a sack about fifteen inches long and eight inches wide. Pale in colour, it was dressed in blood and mucus. She bent forward and tentatively touched it. It felt warm and rubbery, and it moved at her touch.

Frances was too far gone to be afraid. She marvelled at what had come from her womb. She traced her fingers across its surface, making patterns in the blood. She had given birth to an egg. She laughed. Old mother hen had given birth to an egg. She laughed so much her sides ached and tears rolled down her cheeks.

Then she blacked out.

***

It was daylight when Frances woke. Her throat felt dry and an immense pain throbbed between her legs. Her vision was still sleep-blurred, and she felt groggy. Her arms were wrapped around what she thought was a pillow, but when she looked down, she saw that she was cuddling the thing she had given birth to, and she gagged. She couldn't believe it. She thought it had been a nightmare. How on earth could she have given birth to that ... that egg?

Trembling, she snatched her arms back and despite the pain between her legs, she jumped off the bed and scurried away. Cowered in the corner of the room, she looked back at the thing she had spawned.

The empty syringe was on the bed next to it, and she wondered whether the drug was still in her system. Perhaps she was hallucinating. Perhaps she was still asleep. But she knew she wasn't dreaming. Her body was already in too much pain to be asleep.

The egg had felt heavier than it looked, and as she stared at it, she saw it move. Or at least, something inside it moved. Something that was alive.

She felt sick.

The puncture mark on her arm itched, and she scratched it. Scars traced the path of her vein. Some were needle marks, others were insect

68

bites. She knew the little bastards crawled over her at night. Knew they feasted on her blood.

She saw a couple of the little buggers now. Two beetles. They were on the mattress, feasting on the afterbirth that must have slipped out when she was asleep.

Frances saw movement inside the sack. She felt terrified. She had to get rid of it. Destroy it. Whatever she had given birth to was evil.

She walked toward the bed clutching her stomach.

When she reached the mattress, she stared down at the rugby ball shaped object. The thing inside it moved again, more frantically than before. It was as if it sensed what she was about to do.

She crouched and picked it up; held it to her chest. All she had to do was let go, drop it to the floor. She thought it might explode; probably killing whatever was inside, but she couldn't do it.

Despite her loathing of what she had spawned, it was a part of her. She felt it move in her arms. Eyes brimming with tears, she collapsed onto the mattress and rocked her egg.

Phase 2

It had been almost a month since she had given birth, and she had become quite used to pampering her egg. When the first crack appeared several hours earlier, she'd been quite nervous. Now she was excited to see what would come forth.

Despite wanting to help it out, she knew that if it was to have any chance of survival, it had to be able to fend for itself, and as much as it pained her, she waited patiently for the next hour and a half until it finally broke free.

She didn't know what she had expected it to look like, but she never dreamed that it would be green, yellow and black and covered in hairs that twitched as it crawled across the floor. It resembled a caterpillar, but was nearly two feet long. There was something almost humanoid about its face, and as it looked up at Frances, she could have sworn that it was smiling. Frances wiped a tear from her eye. Her baby was beautiful.

"You must be hungry, little one," she said, bending down and stroking its back. The creature arched itself as though enjoying her touch. She didn't know its gender, but there was something masculine about it, so she reasoned that it must be male.

During her time with the oval shell, she had often spoken to it, and she felt that it recognised her voice.

"Well, as you can see, I've left plenty of things for you to chew on." She indicated the rotted food scattered around the room. She didn't even notice the room's horrendous smell anymore. Despite her previous belief that she had not nested, she now knew that she had, only as with everything about her pregnancy, it wasn't conventional. She watched as her baby nudged aside a pile of rotten food, and she felt anxious that it didn't seem to want to eat.

"What's wrong," she asked. She crouched down, picked up some of the food and held it in front of her baby's mouth, but it turned its head away.

She leaned over to pick up another selection of food, and felt her baby nuzzle against her chest. When she looked down, she saw that its mouth had left a wet patch on her shirt.

Since the birth, she had been expressing milk. She never expected to have to breastfeed, but as she unbuttoned her shirt, tugged her bra down and pulled her breast out, it felt like the most natural thing in the world. The baby crawled up onto her lap and latched its mouth around her swollen nipple, making her toes curl. The hairs on its body were slightly irritating, and Frances winced as it began to feed, but slowly the pain subsided and she stroked its head and smiled. Motherhood was the best feeling in the world.

"I suppose we will have to give you a name, won't we little one," she said as it suckled her breast. After a moment, she smiled. "I know, we'll call you, Spike." As if pleased with the name, Spike stopped suckling and looked up at its mother. Its eyes were large and moist, and if she hadn't known better, Frances would have sworn that it smiled back.

Although she loved her baby, she was not foolish enough to broadcast news of the birth. Other people just wouldn't understand. They would probably call Spike an abomination and try to kill him. To Frances, he was a gift. He gave her life purpose.

She hated leaving Spike alone, but her breast milk was not sufficient to feed him, so Frances went back out on the street. Cold winds blew down from the north, and there didn't seem to be as many girls around as before, and so it was easy to satisfy at least ten punters a night.

Even the local dealers seemed to have vanished, and she was having trouble obtaining her supply of Paras. Word on the street was that it was being discontinued due to adverse side affects, and even the dealers didn't want the fallout. Without customers, they had no business so she supposed they thought it was a shrewd move.

She thought she had bought enough to keep her going until she found a new supplier, but now she had run out. After only a couple of days off the drug, Frances was suffering withdrawal symptoms. She seemed to be in a permanent cold sweat. Her hands shook and she had terrible headaches.

If it wasn't for her baby, she didn't think she could continue.

Phase 3

As soon as Frances entered the room, she sensed something was wrong. Normally, Spike would crawl across the ground to meet her, but tonight, he didn't appear. Frances frowned and put down the bag of scraps she had collected from the dustbins behind the Chinese restaurant. She closed the door behind her and switched the light on. A large pupa was hanging from the ceiling. Frances stared at it in amazement.

"Spike, are you in there?" she said. The pupa didn't move. She walked toward it and reached up to run a hand across the surface. It felt dry and brittle, like parchment. "Oh baby, what have you done?" She shook her head and a tear trickled from her eye. Apart from the shortage of Paras, the past four months had been the happiest she could ever remember.

Days passed, and Frances watched the pupa for any sign of her baby, but nothing happened. Days turned into weeks. Between bouts of cold sweat, and when the light was just right, she thought that she could see Spike within the pupa, and she would talk to him, telling him not to be afraid, that it was just another cycle of his life.

She missed her baby so much.

Phase 4

Awoken by a rustling sound, Frances sat up in bed. She strained to see in the dark. Since Spike had been born, she drew the curtains at night in case anyone saw her baby and reported him.

Her body was a lot thinner than it used to be, her wrists like brittle sticks and she had trouble supporting her meagre weight.

Unable to see anything clearly, she struggled to her feet and staggered across the room to switch the light on. Bright light stung her eyes, and she rubbed them with the back of her hands. As her vision cleared, she saw that the pupa had split open, and that it was empty. Behind the empty shell, the curtain wafted in the breeze from the open window.

"Spike, Spike, where are you?" she said.

A rustling sound in the corner of the room drew her attention, and she turned to stare as a three foot horned black beetle waddled across the ground. It had a shiny carapace, six barbed legs and two antennas that twitched in the air. It stopped a few feet from Frances and stared at her, its large proboscis wavering. Its eyes were honeycombed obsidian, flecked with blue. Its shell was segmented. This was not her baby.

Frances wanted to scream. She found the strength to swallow and backed away.

"What have you done to Spike?" she said.

71

The creature tapped a leg on the ground a couple of times and then scuttled closer. Frances jumped back.

"What have you done to my baby?"

The creature twitched its antennas and its mandible opened and closed as if it was trying to communicate.

Aware that she was naked, Frances felt vulnerable. She grabbed a t-shirt from the top of the drawers, and tried to cover her skinny frame. This thing couldn't possibly be her baby, could it? She was unsure what to do.

They stood and stared at each other for a moment, and then the beetle scuttled toward her, reared itself up and stabbed its proboscis into her abdomen like a large hypodermic needle. Frances screamed. It felt like a white hot poker searing her flesh as it pumped something into her body. Next moment she felt a familiar warm feeling penetrate her system

The beetle withdrew, and she watched as its carapace parted to reveal wings. It flapped them a couple of times. Then it crawled up to the window, nudged the curtain aside, leaned out and flew off into the night.

She smiled. Children leave the nest so young these days, she thought.

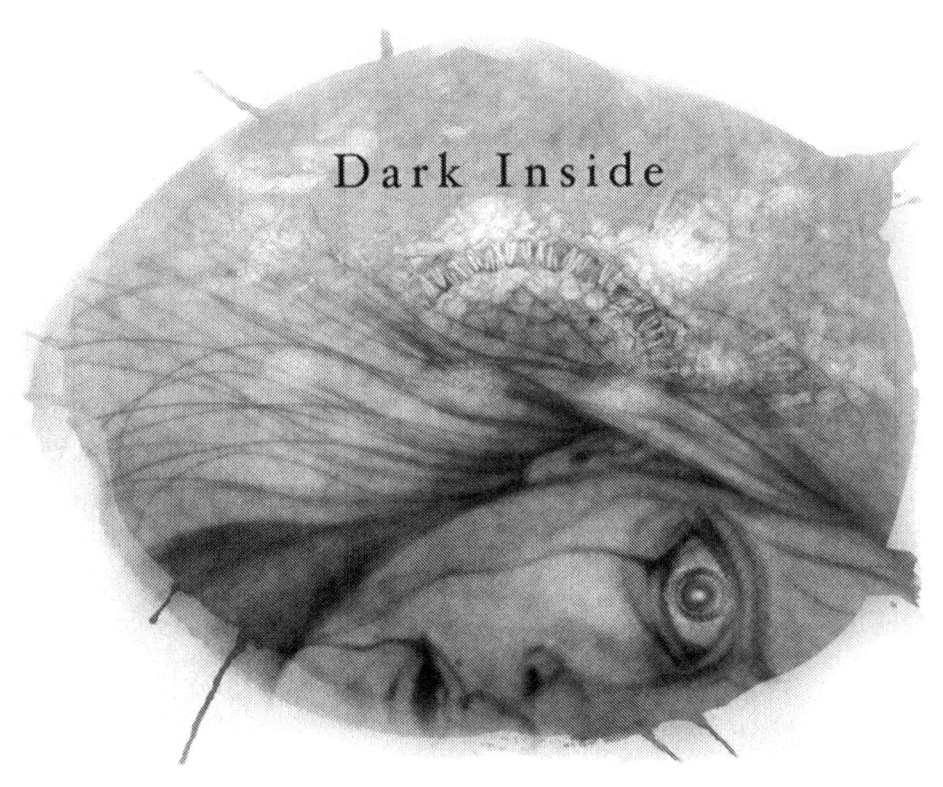

Dark Inside

I once thought dying was the worst that could happen.

Then I came back ...

10.15 a.m. – July 18

Stood on the bow of the cruise ship, Silver Surf, I performed my best impression of Leonardo DiCaprio from the film, Titanic.

"I'm the king of the world," I shouted, much to my little brother's amusement. He covered his mouth with his hand and giggled. The sea breeze animated his mop of sandy coloured hair like a strange sea anemone. I think it amused him more because I'm his sister; everything I do makes him laugh.

I liked making him laugh.

A couple of passengers looked at me with distaste, perhaps thinking my reference to a film concerning an ill-fated liner inappropriate, but they could go swivel.

The wind had messed my long blonde hair, and as I stepped away from the bow I brushed a strand out of my eyes and hooked it behind my ear. The sea breeze had made my eyes water slightly and the ship's structure offered only relative protection.

If the truth be told, I hadn't been looking forward to the holiday. It was my parents' idea; I imagined the ship would be like an old people's home. But luckily my preconceptions had been wrong as there were a number of young people onboard and to my surprise and relief I had enjoyed it so far. There was plenty to do. The ship had two showrooms, a sports court, four swimming pools, library, pizzeria, steakhouse, casino, hamburger grill and shops galore. A floating town, inhabited by 1,950 passengers and crew.

Out of the passengers, one boy in particular had caught my eye. Tanned and sporty with short brown hair, he looked drop-dead gorgeous and I felt sure he would pluck up the courage to speak to me – if he didn't, then I would have to make the first move. Life's too short to miss out.

"What's that?" Jake asked, bringing me out of my reverie.

I looked where he was pointing and saw a small boat floating in our path. Although difficult to see clearly from our position and distance, it looked abandoned.

Noticing a steward nearby, I called him over and pointed the boat out. He thanked me for my keen eye, and hurried away to report the vessel.

Even though I knew it took a mile to stop the ship, it wasn't long before I felt us slowing, and I watched as they launched a boat to investigate Jake's sighting.

10.57 a.m.

The unscheduled slowing of the ship generated a lot of interest, and by the time the launch returned, towing the small boat, a number of people had gathered on the deck to watch.

Hard to see clearly from where we stood, I grabbed Jake's hand and led him through the crowd and down to where I imagined they would dock (I had seen hatches in the lower decks that were used to ferry supplies from the islands). In the back of my mind, I remembered something about a person who saves property at sea being entitled to a reward, and as Jake spotted it first, I felt any reward should come his way.

11.24 a.m.

When we arrived, a great deal of commotion came from the men gathered around the boat. I don't know why, but my heart felt like a punch bag under attack.

"Hey, what do you kids think you're doing here?"

I turned to face a gruff looking man with a bald head and a pockmarked face. Being called a kid really annoyed me. I'm 16, but I think I look older. My figure often draws admiring glances, and the bikini top I wore today only just covered my breasts.

"It was my brother and me that spotted the boat," I said. As I spoke, I noticed the gaze of his grey eyes stray toward my bosom, and then quickly realign with my face.

"Well, you're not meant to be down here. It's dangerous."

Before I had a chance to reply, someone shouted and we all turned to look at the boat that had been dragged aboard.

Another shout rang out. People fell back, stumbling over one another, and what looked like a black blanket suddenly flowed over the side of the boat.

I frowned, and then opened my mouth in shock as I realised that it was a plague of rats ... and they were running toward me. They scurried quickly across the deck, and then without warning, one of them launched itself at me, and I felt its sharp little teeth sink into my arm.

But it was the sight of a man hauling human bones out of the boat that made me scream.

12.13 p.m.

I could tell as the doctor stuck the needle into my arm that he enjoyed inflicting pain. I winced, which caused a faint smile to break the straight countenance of his narrow lips. He had a face like granite rock, weather-beaten, upon which the smile seemed ill at ease.

"That antibiotic should help ward off any infection," he said.

My mother sat at my side, shaking her head. "What the hell were you doing there anyway?" she asked for the umpteenth time.

I sighed, tired of explaining myself. The pulsing throb of a headache didn't help.

People always commented that I acquired my good looks from my mother. At the moment, her blue eyes looked close to tears, although I didn't know whether through anger or concern. Her hair was as blonde as mine, but shorter. We also shared the same little button nose, and I think my bosom will be as plentiful too. The T-shirt she bought during our stop in Jamaica made her look cheap. Two sizes too small, it bared her midriff and the pierced belly button she had done last year. It's time she grew up.

My father sat behind her with his back against the wall. He seemed distracted; his thoughts probably on the state of his car components business back home. I don't think he wanted to come on this holiday; I probably inherited my mother's stubborn streak, too.

13.20 p.m.

By now I felt awful. A headache thumped away inside my skull like a demonic parasite and a fever made me feel delirious. Mother sent for the doctor, but it appeared that I was not the only one to have been bitten by the rats, and he was busy elsewhere.

Although I couldn't be sure, I think my mother's more worried than she's letting on. I heard her whispering to my father (which is never a good sign), and they won't let Jake in to see me.

17.30 p.m.

Time felt as though it had stopped. The last few hours seemed to have dragged on for days. I think I've been sleeping, but I'm not sure.

"But she's only sixteen; she can't be dead," my mother said.

I wondered briefly who my mother was referring to, and I tried to turn my head to ask, but I couldn't move.

Panicked, I tried to open my mouth to speak, to cry out, but I couldn't. I couldn't do anything.

A shadow moved into my field of view, and the doctor's face appeared above me like the angel of death. He shook his head and then closed my eyelids. Dark inside, I felt strangely numb.

"I'm sorry, Mrs Hoyle."

My mother screamed.

I wanted to open my eyes; wanted to scream back that I wasn't dead, but I couldn't. My mouth and eyes remained glued shut.

In the background, I heard the captain's voice come over the Tannoy.

"Ladies and gentlemen, as you know, a few hours after leaving Haiti, we picked up a vessel that was floating adrift. Unfortunately, the vessel was harbouring a quantity of rats that have now entered the ship. These rats have bitten a number of people, and it has been found that the rats are carrying an unidentified virus. You are advised not to leave your cabins until further notice. But rest assured that we are doing everything in our power to contain the situation."

Virus. The word made me think back to a recent biology class. Virus: any of a group of sub microscopic entities capable of replication only within the cells of animals and plants.

That didn't sound too good. As I contemplated my predicament, I heard more voices in the room, strange voices, and although I couldn't move, I felt them lift my body and carry me through the ship.

I heard people talking in the background; some cried. Far away, I heard a scream.

19.02 p.m.

When I opened my eyes, the darkness didn't fade; it took me a moment to realise that something rested lightly on my face. I instinctively reached up, glad that my ability to move had returned, and tugged off what turned out to be a white, linen sheet. Light from a bare bulb above cast a veil of luminescence, revealing the room to be some sort of storage facility piled high with boxes.

Before I fell into what I can only assume was a coma, I had felt someone touching me up. I had wanted to scream at them to stop, but of course I couldn't. To all intents and purposes I was dead. That's what made it so sickening. I don't know how far the person would have gone if they weren't interrupted by someone entering the room and announcing another dead body needed collecting – I couldn't help but think that it had been doctor death copping a quick feel.

I now felt hungry. Ravenous. It not only manifested itself as a burning sensation in my stomach, but as an overpowering urge to feast.

I sat up. My body felt different, my muscle fibres tighter, as if they had contracted, and my skin felt leathery. Red blotches marred my arms; where the blood had pooled my body looked bruised. I probably looked as bad as I felt.

Swinging my legs over the side of the trolley, I stood up and then almost collapsed. At first, walking proved difficult; I felt reborn, having to learn all over.

There were other bodies in the room, but I sensed that they too weren't dead, that we had been pricked like Sleeping Beauty and had fallen asleep. But no Prince came to awaken us.

19.21 p.m.

Upon leaving the room, my family came to mind. It took a while to get my bearings, but once I did, I made my way back to the cabin we shared.

The ship seemed unnaturally quiet. In the distance, I heard the slap of waves against the bow, and felt the steady throb of the engines vibrating through the floor. My whole body felt attuned.

20.01 p.m.

When I reached the cabin, I opened the door without hesitating.

My mother sat with her head in her hands; she looked up when I entered. Mascara marred her face in tearful lines.

Her expression transformed through surprise, pleasure and finally, shock.

Then she screamed.

It's hard to say what I felt at that moment. Any other time I would have been saddened to have seen her so upset. Now ...

With no sign of Father and Jake, I guessed they were out somewhere. Perhaps father was trying to explain the concept of death to my brother, but he would be ill-informed.

I opened my mouth and tried to speak, but no words would come – at least nothing that sounded intelligible.

Impelled to move, I staggered forward and grabbed my mother. Apparently too shocked to stir, she gurgled something as incoherent as my own effort at communication, but I wasn't really listening. I needed to quench the burning in my stomach.

I sank my teeth into mother's neck and clamped them together and ripped out a chunk of flesh as sweet as any prime steak. Mother gurgled something and for a brief moment, she struggled. But it was futile. Death had empowered me.

It felt almost karmic – seemed only right that mother nurtured me in death as she had in life.

20.34 p.m.

Sated for now, I sat in the darkness, cradling my mothers severed arm. I didn't feel any guilt. I didn't feel anything.

I sensed the others like me, rising from their dead sleep — felt it through a primal connection that united us in death.

Footsteps echoed outside the door and then stopped; the handle started to turn. I heard voices: my father and brother. I would never make Jake laugh again.

Soon, everyone would be dark inside ...

Clockwork

I knew the black cat was dead. Even if I hadn't just seen it struck by the car, I would still know it was dead. Finding my father lying on the floor two weeks ago, hands clutched to his chest as though trying to keep warm made sure of that.

One of the cat's front paws protruded at an odd angle, its claws protracted as if in a failed attempt to scratch at the vehicle that had bowled it along the road.

The driver of the car hadn't stopped. Unlike dogs, you didn't have to report it if you killed a cat.

I gingerly reached out and touched the body. Its fur still felt warm and soft. My fingers brushed a red collar around its neck. The attached tag on the collar told me the cat was called Sooty.

Although it was only a cat, I couldn't stand the thought of the owner finding the dead feline in or at the side of the road, so I picked the carcass up, and with nowhere else to put it, I dropped it in with the shopping I had bought in town. I would bury it when I reached home.

A car drove by, making me flinch. I wondered what it sounded like; wondered what lots of things sounded like. Deaf since birth, I lived in a world of unimaginable silence. The only time I had been glad of my deafness was when I saw mother screaming after I alerted her to father's body.

***

When I arrived home, I reached into the bag and touched the cat. Its body now cold, it had already started to go stiff. I stroked it once, and then opened the gate and deposited the corpse outside my den at the bottom of the garden before heading toward the house.

"You took your time," mother said as she took the shopping bags from me. She enunciated each word so I could lip-read.

I shrugged and signed that I had lost track of time.

Mother smiled, but she couldn't disguise the haunted look of the bereaved. She started to say something else, but her lips stopped moving and she pulled out a tin of baked beans dotted with blood. She frowned. "What's this?"

Already one-step ahead, I weaved my fingers to say the steaks must have leaked.

Mother nodded. It was a reasonable answer, as the cuts of meat often leaked.

My sister, Vicky, sat in her highchair, playing with a rattle. I smiled at her and she smiled back. She opened and closed her mouth and I touched her cheek, feeling the vibrations of noise resonating through her skin. While mother put the shopping away, I made my way out to the den, a wooden structure four foot high and three foot square that I had built last summer.

The cat lay on the grass outside. If it weren't for the mangled paw and the specks of blood, it would look as though it were having a catnap.

I picked it up, opened the door and carried it into the den, stooping as I entered.

It was warm inside the room, and I stood up straight. Sheets of plastic yellowed in the sun made the light that shone through the window appear golden, illuminating the clocks that covered every surface.

There were mechanical clocks, pendulum clocks, mantel clocks, cuckoo clocks and clocks that I had made. Within the den, I could feel the reverberating beat of the clocks like a huge heart, and feeling the familiar tick-tock of the clocks through the ground and walls, I felt it was the closest I came to actually hearing.

Pieces of clocks cluttered the table against the back wall. There were springs, cogs, levers, weights and a whole host of other parts. I swept some of the bits aside and deposited the cat on the table while I searched for a bag to put it in. Deciding on an old plastic one, I turned back and grabbed the cat. Straight away, I felt the familiar pulse of the clocks through my fingers. For a brief moment, I imagined the cat was still alive, that I had made a mistake, that it wasn't dead.

A coiled spring unwound against the cat's leg. I stared at the clock components. If there was one thing I was good at, it was making broken things work again. And that's when the idea came to mind. What if I could mend the cat? I wasn't thinking I could bring it back to life, but perhaps I could give it a semblance of life, could give it movement.

I thought about it for a long while before I actually set to work.

There was a penknife on the table. I picked it up and unfastened the blade, feeling it click open. A thin sheen of sweat painted my brow as I gingerly held the small penknife against the cat's soft underbelly. This was stupid. I couldn't do it, and my stomach recoiled at the thought.

With a shake of my head, I dropped the knife and stared at the corpse. It looked pitiful and fresh tears stung my eyes. After a slight hesitation, I picked the knife up again and sliced the blade into the cat before I had time to change my mind. It wasn't so bad when I started. There wasn't much blood as no heart pumped, and despite the cold, slimy feel, removing the cat's innards was no worse than taking the giblets out of the turkey at Christmas, something I had done last year.

Once I had gutted the cat, I started to construct a mechanism to provide movement. It wouldn't be the most technical of accomplishments, but I knew when it was inside the cat, no one would see it, so I wasn't too concerned with its aesthetics. I used a small drill to make holes in the cat's bones, to which I attached Meccano strips, supplementing its own skeleton with one of my own onto which I attached the clockwork device I had made.

I had to make a couple of journeys to the house, but mother seemed to either not notice me or ignore me as she fed Vicky.

Because I found the body, I think she blames me for father's death.

It took the best part of the remainder of the day, but eventually I finished.

I stood the cat on the table, inserted a key into a small hole in its underside and turned it. Through my fingers on the cat's back I could feel the cogs turning, the multiple springs being tensioned.

Ten turns later, I released the key and stepped back. The cat's eyes stared back at me, but nothing happened.

Wondering if I had done something wrong, I stepped toward the cat when it suddenly blinked, stopping me in my tracks. That wasn't supposed to happen. Its eyes weren't supposed to blink; couldn't blink because nothing powered them. I had considered how to make its eyes move, but decided making it walk would be enough.

The cat's head moved a fraction, just a twitch at first, almost imperceptible, then it swivelled from side to side as though testing the movement. It took a tentative step, its movement's jerky, mechanical. The limbs hardly bent at the joints, which was disappointing after I'd spent so long fashioning the Meccano and bone links.

I could feel my heart beating in time with the clocks that pulsed through the room. The cat staggered toward me, its limbs moving with the stiffness of a soldier on parade. I took a step back; could feel the blood throbbing at my temples, could feel the sweat on my back.

What had I done?

The cat opened its mouth. That shouldn't have happened either. It wasn't wired to work.

I wondered whether it made a sound.

Unable to look at it any longer, I ran out of the den, back to the house and into the kitchen where I stood shaking.

"Alex, are you okay?" mother asked as she looked up from feeding Vicky.

I couldn't tell her what I'd done, didn't fully understand it enough to explain, but that dead cat was more than a reanimated clockwork pussy. It had a life of its own, and it terrified me. I'd only wanted to make it move, to make it not seem so dead.

"You're pale as a sheet. Are you sure you're okay?"

I signed that I was fine, then I offered to carry on feeding Vicky while mother had a break. Mother smiled and nodded.

"You're a good boy, Alex."

While I spoon-fed Vicky something purporting to be pasta in sauce, I thought about the cat. I couldn't leave it in the den. But what could I do with it?

My sister opened and closed her mouth, as greedy as a baby bird. Her hair was like spun gold, her eyes as blue as the sky. She still had a lot of baby fat, which made her look like those old paintings of cherubs. I smiled at her, and she smiled back. I envied her the innocence that didn't yet feel the pain of loss.

After I'd fed and changed her, I rocked her to sleep, put her in the cot and then walked back out to the den.

I stood outside the structure, my hand on the door, feeling the beat of the clocks through the wood.

Bracing myself, I took a deep breath, then flung the door open and stepped back. When the cat didn't appear, I took a cautious step toward the den and peered inside to find the cat had torn its way through the plastic window.

Distressed, I ran around the side of the den and looked in the hedgerows to see if I could spot the cat, but it was nowhere to be seen.

How far would it get with ten winds of the key?

Surely not that far.

I remembered the way it had blinked and opened its mouth, actions it wasn't supposed to be able to do. Perhaps it would go further than I imagined. Perhaps the clockwork components weren't powering it at all; perhaps it hadn't really been dead. A shiver ran up my spine. I felt like screaming but didn't know if it was through fear or uncertainty.

Although I continued searching, there was no sign of the cat. After a while, I even wondered whether it had really happened, but when I returned to the den, I noticed the cat's innards in the plastic bag that I'd put them in. They had started to smell so I buried them in the garden and then ran back inside the house, where I shut and bolted the door.

***

During the next few days, I stayed indoors more than normal, which didn't go unnoticed by mother. I think she preferred it when I was out. She questioned me a couple of times, and I could tell she thought there was something wrong. But I couldn't tell her what I had done as it didn't seem right. Besides, I didn't think she'd believe me.

That first night in bed, I had felt sure the cat was going to creep up on me, and there I'd be, unable to hear it. So I lay on the mattress in a way that I could touch the floor, trying to feel for the tick-tock of my feline creation, but when it never came, I eventually fell asleep.

It wasn't until three days later that I found the bird's carcass in the hedgerow.

I stared at it for a while, wondering how it had died. Eventually, I crouched down and picked the bird up, recognised it as a starling. When I looked closer, I noticed a hole in its neck. Parting the plumage around the hole, I could just make out the shuttlecock ridges of an air rifle pellet.

Bird in hand, I walked down to the den. Being a small creature made it a tricky process, but I made a small incision on the underside of its chest. Into this, I placed a small frame, to which I attached the motor, fashioned from watches. Its legs were too small to animate, so I didn't consider doing anything other than making its wings move. I hoped it would be enough.

I had rigged the windup mechanism into its chest, and I gave the key ten turns and then set the bird on the table.

It took a while, but then it blinked and its beak opened and closed. It flexed its wings, the movement still very mechanical. Moments later, the bird gave a nod of its head and launched itself into the air. It made an ungainly test flight, struggling to keep itself airborne. I wondered whether the watch components were too heavy.

It finally came to rest on the windowsill where it fluttered its wings a couple of times before flying away through the open door.

I ran outside and watched it struggle into the sky, circling higher and higher until I lost sight of it. When I eventually lowered my gaze, I saw mother standing at the back door, gazing out. She looked happy; Vicky babbled in her arms.

***

When I found Vicky sprawled on the floor by her highchair a couple of days later, it seemed like an ironic case of déjà vu. I stared at her for a moment, then checked her neck for a pulse. The feel of her cold skin made me flinch. I sat back and chewed a fingernail, wondering whether she had cried out when she fell. Not that it would have mattered as I wouldn't have heard.

Having left Vicky in my care while she visited my father's grave, mother would undoubtedly hold me responsible. This time she would be right.

My sister felt heavier than she was as I lifted her from the floor and carried her out to the den. The partially gutted badger that I had been working on eyed me from the bench as I set my sister down. My skill at reanimating the clockwork menagerie had grown immeasurably.

I picked up the knife.

Hopefully, mother would never notice.

Venetian Kiss

"It looks as if we go through this square and along a few alleys," Alex said, shoving the map of Venice into the back pocket of his jeans.

"Are you sure?" Jade asked, only too aware her fiancé wasn't known for his directional skills, having gotten lost more times than she cared to remember.

Alex wore a mock frown, but his blue eyes spoiled the effect as they twinkled with mischief. His short, dark hair was still tussled from the boat trip from Marco Polo Airport. Jade considered her own long blondee hair must look equally windswept.

The boat ride had certainly been exhilarating, and she didn't think there was a better way to arrive in the city of romance, landing near Piazza San Marco, with the impressive dome of the Santa Maria della Salute church situated at the entrance to the Grand Canal to their left.

The tourists bustling around the quay looked at the world through the eye of a lens, photographing everything in sight. From the pictures she had seen in books, Jade recognised the Doge's Palace, Saint Mark's Cathedral, the clock tower and a column with a golden lion standing guard on top. The only thing that spoiled the scene was the inclement weather and the pigeons. They were everywhere; the beat of their wings when they took flight en masse sounded like thunder.

As they made their way through the bustle of tourists in the Piazza San Marco, Jade noticed a dead pigeon like a sacrificial offering at the base of the column supporting the lion. Other pigeons pecked at it and Jade wondered whether they were trying to revive it or eat it; either way it unnerved her slightly - are pigeons carnivorous? she wondered.

Classical music emanated from somewhere; it seemed fitting in the ancient surrounds. Many of the people were dressed for the carnival: harlequins in diamond patterned outfits and black masks, people in white costumes with diagonal green stripes and green masks with broken noses — a whole range of wondrous disguises.

Suddenly the hairs prickled on the nape of her neck and she turned to see a sexless, white masked figure leaning nonchalantly against a column, staring at her with dark, soulless eyes. The figure was dressed in 18th century attire, with a short cape and a black, cocked hat. The figure doffed his hat, bowed and then disappeared into the crowd.

She didn't know why, but the stranger unnerved her. The eyes had looked hungry, almost predatory.

"This way," Alex said, picking up the suitcase and lumbering away.

Jade was about to follow when she noticed water bubbling through holes in the stone paving.

"What's happening?" she asked, her expression one of panic.

Alex laughed. "It's only the tide coming in. Don't worry, we won't drown."

Jade gave him a playful punch on the arm. "OK wise guy, just remember who's got the passports. You don't want to get stuck here, do you?"

"Oh, I don't know," he replied, staring over her shoulder.

Jade turned to see what had drawn his gaze and spotted a group of teenage girls dressed in shorts and crop-tops. Although she was dressed in jeans and a jumper, she felt cold just looking at them. "As long as looking's all you do," she said.

Alex winked. "You know there's only room in my heart for you."

Jade rolled her eyes and tutted in mock exasperation.

He looked back at the girls. "But I could always take in lodgers."

Jade punched him again, harder this time.

Alex flinched. "Ow. You know I was only joking."

Jade suddenly winced as a sharp pain pricked her calf. She bent down and scratched the afflicted area, aggravating the pain. Rolling the leg of her jeans up, she saw a small red blotch on the surface of her skin.

"Damn mosquitoes."

Alex frowned. "I didn't think they were active at this time of year."

"Well, tell that to the little blood sucker that did this."

"That must be what they call a Venetian kiss; they must like the taste of you."

"Well the feeling's not mutual." She scratched at the area again, inflaming it further.

"You'll only make it worse if you do that."

"Thank you for the advice, Doctor," she said, rankled at being bitten on the first day of her holiday. To make matters worse, she hadn't even packed any bug spray - she hadn't thought she would need it. "Come on, let's get to the hotel before they come back for seconds."

Alex sniggered and continued toward one of the many alleys. Jade sulked along behind him like a shadow; she didn't appreciate his lack of concern for her pain, and she realised that three months wasn't long enough to know anyone very well, never mind to start planning marriage.

The gloomy alleys harboured numerous shops full of local Murano glassware, masks, jewellery and leather goods. Sightseers still walked the paths, but as they strayed far from the main tourist traps, they weren't as abundant, the streets far quieter and eerie.

The buildings leaned over them, almost predatory, the brickwork painted in muted reds and yellows. Small bridges crossed over the murky green canals, the buildings that fronted the water partly submerged and coated with a dirty residue where the tide rose and fell.

The occasional gondola sailed by, the gondoliers - who had joined in the festivities by dressing in costumes - ducking as they passed beneath the low bridges, their poles dredging the murky depths of the water.

As they walked over a narrow bridge, Jade heard a scream and she flinched. The oppressive shadows made it seem as though the dark clouds had descended to the streets and alleys. She tried to trace the source of the sound, but couldn't see anyone - all she could hear was the dull, ghostly echo of their own footsteps.

"Did you hear that?" she asked.

Alex shrugged, indifferent.

The next minute, Jade heard heavy footsteps approaching. The sound was ominous in the pervasive atmosphere of the deserted alley and she caught up with Alex and gripped his hand tightly.

Someone screamed again and Jade's heart missed a beat as a girl ran from around the corner of a building. Half her face was hidden behind a dark mask; her eyes shone like diamonds, her lips a blood red gash. She wore a long cloak that flapped around her naked torso like a large wing, allowing her breasts to swing free.

Another figure emerged behind her, features hidden behind a sinister red mask with a long, beaked nose; the girl glanced over her shoulder and screamed again.

Jade's heart thundered and goose bumps erupted along her arms like a rash.

As the girl ran past Jade, the scream became a laugh - they were playing some sort of game. Jade shook her head and sighed in relief. Although it was carnival time, she certainly hadn't expected to see half naked people running around.

When she looked at Alex, she noticed he was standing with his mouth open, watching the couple until they disappeared into the maze of alleys.

"Have you seen enough?" Jade said, frowning. "Or would you like to get the camera out and take their photo?"

Alex grinned. "Sorry, but it's not every day you see a half naked girl running through the streets."

"Good thing, otherwise your eyes and jaw would stick like that." Although she tried to make light of the situation, Jade found it disconcerting. People shouldn't be allowed to run through the streets like that. It wasn't decent. Not that she was a prude, but running through the streets half undressed seemed improper.

Alex smiled and nodded. "Well, when in Rome ..." He undid the top two buttons of his blue shirt.

"Don't even think about it, buster. Besides, this is Venice. Rome is a few hundred miles south of here." She cocked a thumb, indicating what she perceived to be south.

"It was worth a try if it meant getting naked."

Jade shook her head and rolled her eyes. "Do you know where we are?" she asked, changing the subject.

"Trust me, we must be nearly there."

Jade wasn't convinced. It hadn't looked this far on the map, otherwise she would have asked the water-taxi driver if he could take them straight to the hotel. It was Alex's idea to walk. He said it would help them get a feel for the place, but the only feelings she had at the moment were the aching ones in her feet and the Venetian kiss that throbbed on her calf.

"Well, could I have a look at the map?"

"Don't you trust me?" He looked hurt, and she didn't know whether it was the dark atmosphere, but the twinkle in his eyes now seemed slightly sinister and lecherous.

"Just let me look at the map." Why didn't he ever do what she asked?

"You'll have to catch me first." He took the map out of the back pocket of his jeans and waved it tauntingly in the air.

"Grow up. I only want a look."

Alex laughed, turned around and started running away, the suitcase banging against his leg.

"Jesus, Alex, what are you playing at?" she shouted.

"If you want it, you'll have to catch me," he replied from the shadows into which he had disappeared.

Biting her bottom lip, Jade strode after him. She wasn't going to give him the satisfaction of running. This was a side of him she had never seen before and she didn't like it.

A gondola appeared from beneath a bridge, the gondolier hunched over as he propelled the craft through the confined space.

He doffed his feather-plumed cap as he drew near. His face was hidden behind a ghastly, yellow mask and he wore a purple, velvet costume with a large ruff that made his head look as though it was on a platter.

"Buon giorno," the gondolier said as he brought his craft to a stop.

Jade nodded and smiled nervously. She found not being able to see peoples' faces unnerving. On a whim, she decided to ask if he knew where the hotel was, and she enunciated each word as though speaking to a child.

The gondolier nodded his head and gestured to his gondola. "Please, I take you."

She considered refusing, but her feet ached and she would like to see Alex's face when he saw her sail by on a gondola. She took the phrase book out of her shoulder bag to ask the price. "Quanto costa?"

The gondolier shook his head. "Prego, prego. Don't worry pretty lady. For you, niente. Nothing. You are fresh, yes?"

Jade stifled a laugh at his wrong use of word. Like a typical, ignorant tourist, she thought she would have to use the universal language of pointing and gesturing to communicate her ideas and needs, and she found her ignorance embarrassing. "How did you know I was new to Venice?"

The gondolier shrugged expressively. "It's easy, pretty lady. You is lost." His voice sounded oddly distorted, which she assumed was due to the mask.

Jade frowned. "Is it that obvious?"

"Only lost people ever come here."

Here! Did he mean Venice, or was his meaning lost in the translation? Sighing, Jade had to admit she was lost. And even with the map, she knew Alex was too. Damn it, why was he behaving like a jerk? How could he leave her in a strange city, running away like that? "Are you sure I don't have to pay you anything?"

The gondolier shook his head. "This is carnival. Your beautiful company would please me, and is payment enough if you smile for me."

Laughing, Jade stepped to the edge of the canal and ran a hand through her hair. She looked at the pea green water and then at the gondolier. What could it hurt?

The gondolier reached out a hand, and she accepted, surprised at how cold and bony it felt, and stepped down into the gondola. The vessel rocked slightly as she took her seat, and she felt slightly nervous as there wasn't much distance between her and the murky green water. The gondolier stood behind her, and he pushed off with his pole, letting the gondola drift away from the stone bank, the craft swaying slightly as he propelled them along.

Some of the towering buildings lining the canal had half submerged windows and doors, the lower levels flooded. Other buildings had window boxes; the trailing plants withered and dead like skeletal bones. Rusty balconies adorned a few buildings, the supporting pillars covered in grime; but she had to admit there was a surreal beauty to the place.

Noticing small, bronze wolf heads on either side of the gondola, Jade shivered. It wasn't what she would have chosen for decoration.

A building loomed out of the pervasive shadows. A darker area sat over the water like a gaping maw, and she realised it was a tunnel stretching under the building, and that they were heading toward it.

She stared along the paths either side of the canal, looking for Alex. She had hoped to spot him so she could laugh and poke fun as she sailed past, but when she didn't see him, and knowing how useless his sense of direction was, she decided she had better go back and look for him.

"Excuse me, but I think I'd better get out," she said.

When the gondola failed to slow its smooth passage through the water, she turned to voice her request again, but what she saw made her gasp.

Revealed in a patch of light, the gondolier's hands looked like claws. She tried to assure herself it was a trick of the light, or some part of his costume, but she wasn't convinced.

"Can you drop me off here," she asked, her voice wavering.

"Don't worry, pretty lady," the gondolier whispered, propelling them toward the tunnel.

A cold dread crept over Jade and without knowing why, she screamed. Although the canal wasn't very wide, she didn't think she could jump to the bank - the water looked too rancid and she didn't fancy falling in. The next minute, they sailed into the tunnel beneath the building and her scream petered out. The darkness was absolute, like passing through a door to the underworld, and Jade's breath hitched in her throat. She heard water dripping onto the surface of the canal; felt it splash on her face. At least she hoped it was water; her mind conjured disturbing images.

Although she couldn't see the gondolier, she sensed him and heard his ragged breath. "Please, just take me back," she said.

"You were lost, pretty lady, now you is found," he said huskily.

Something brushed against Jade's face and she flinched. It felt cold, like dead flesh and she let out a small yelp. A rancid smell filled the air, clung to the back of her throat like a leech.

A faint, grey patch of light seeped across the walls up ahead.

Moments later, they drifted out of the tunnel, and Jade jumped to her feet. Her sudden movement caused the gondola to sway violently, and she held her arms out to steady herself. Spying the bank, she braced herself - it was about three feet away, and she bit her lip. She absently registered voices, and she considered shouting for help, but she needed to get onto dry land first. Steeling herself, she took a deep breath and launched herself toward the bank. The distance between gondola and bank narrowed as if in slow motion, and the next minute her feet hit solid ground. She felt a moment of exhilaration. She had made it without falling into the water.

Hoping to spot an exit, she stared around what appeared to be the bowels of the building. The walls were bare bricks, slimy in appearance and various tunnels branched off, catacomb tributaries that allowed the canal to continue. Pillars supported the high vaulted ceiling, the illumination provided by hundreds of candles, the flames from which flickered, casting morbid shadows. Looking toward where the voices emanated, she was about to shout for help, but she hesitated.

The crowd were dressed in various, outlandish clothes, grotesque caricatures who wore an assortment of masks: oval, round, square, flat; ones with beaked noses, flat noses, no noses; ones with feather head-dresses, ones covered in leaves, gold ones, white ones, multicoloured ones, all manner of designs.

She turned, spotted the gondolier mooring his vessel. Once he finished, he stood up straight and turned to face Jade. Then with great deliberation, he removed his mask.

Jade screamed so loud her throat hurt.

The gondolier's face was grotesque, inhuman, and worse than any mask imaginable. Instead of flesh, he seemed to have scales that reflected a rainbow of muted colours across its surface. His fleshy, fishlike lips peeled back to reveal small, sharp teeth and he gazed at her hungrily, his bulbous eyes looking about ready to pop out of their sockets.

Jade turned, terrified, hoping to seek help from the crowd; she thought she was losing her mind.

"Jesus, help me," she screamed.

The assembly turned to face her, removing their masks as they did so to reveal their own, monstrous faces - faces moulded by nightmares. Jade felt trapped.

She stumbled away, legs shaking uncontrollably and her heart beating an SOS. A sick feeling bubbled in her stomach and she whirled back to face the gondolier.

"It's hard for us to walk among you unseen," the gondolier said. "But during carnival ..."

"What do you want with me?" Jade screamed.

The gondolier offered a vicious grin and Jade heard Alex's voice in her head: That must be what they call a Venetian kiss; they must like the taste of you.

She screamed again, louder, longer and harder. And then she ran. Ran past the gondolier toward one of the catacomb tunnels as fast as her legs would carry her. A narrow walkway ran alongside the canal, providing just enough room for one person to traverse. The light from the candles radiated a short way along the tunnel, and then darkness encroached.

She heard footsteps in pursuit, and her heart danced a fandango in her chest.

What the hell was going on?

Breathing in short, quick bursts, her lungs laboured with the exertion - they felt like bellows pumping a furnace.

She felt intense fear, as keen as a knife.

What were these ... things?

Growls emanated from the shadows, guttural and menacing sounds that echoed along the arterial tunnel.

Using the wall as a guide, she moved through the dark, grimacing at the slimy brickwork, her eyes wide as she tried to perceive where she was. But it was no good. The darkness was absolute.

She glanced over her shoulder, and then wished she hadn't. Multitudinous eyes glistened in the dark like strange creatures rising from the dark depths of the ocean, winking in and out of existence as the monsters blinked. She wanted to scream again, but she knew she needed to conserve her strength for flight.

Her legs ached, her thighs burning.

Something dripped on her face, gelatinous and rancid and she gagged at the vile odour.

Then she saw a beacon of light ahead and she ran toward it, coming out into a massive, subterranean room. What she saw made her gag. Sharp pains stabbed at her stomach.

Stinking carcasses in various stages of decay decorated the room.

A group of monsters sat hunched around the bodies, feasting, tearing off strips of human flesh and ripping out chunks of tender meat. A couple of the creatures gnawed at ribs, while others delved clawed appendages into the entrails, slurping them up like obscene spaghetti. As Jade entered the room, they looked up and grinned salaciously.

As the monsters started toward her, Jade spotted another passage and ducked inside. At first she thought it was a dead end: all she could see was murky water and her heart sank. But then she saw a chink of light reflected below the surface, and her spirits soared as she realised that it must be a flooded passage that led to one of the partly submerged doors and windows she had seen from the gondola.

As the monsters approached, she didn't hesitate. She jumped into the canal. The water was freezing and she recoiled as though electrocuted. Trying to control her panic, she ducked beneath the water and swam toward the source of the light. Her lungs felt about ready to burst and her arms and legs flailed uselessly, but it was working, the light getting closer and brighter.

When she reached the source, she found it was a window, the glass green with algae. Bracing herself, she smashed her elbow through the panes and ignoring the shark's teeth shards, she swam through and kicked her legs to propel herself up.

A second later, she broke the surface and gulped for breath. It was the sweetest thing she had ever tasted.

With a couple of strokes, she reached the bank and dragged herself ashore. A group of Japanese tourists stared at her. Apparently too aghast to take the obligatory photograph, they pointed and stared.

"Down there," she said through chattering teeth, "down there, monsters!"

The Japanese tourists looked at her with puzzled frowns. Realising they didn't understand a word she was saying, and that the universal language of pointing wasn't going to work, Jade staggered away.

Carnival revellers lingered at every corner, and she snuck past, hugging the shadows as best she could. Who knew what lurked beneath the harlequins disguise?

When she saw people that weren't in costume, she asked them for directions to the hotel, ignoring their questions about her dishevelled appearance. She didn't think they would believe her if she told them the truth.

Hurrying over a small bridge, she suddenly spotted Alex standing on the other side, puzzling over the map. She ran toward him and flung her arms around his neck.

"Jade, where the hell have you been?"

"We need to get out of here," she said, speaking so fast the words ran together, almost unintelligible.

Alex pulled away. "You're soaking wet. What's happened?"

"Look just trust me, we've got to get out of here."

"What's wrong?"

Jade took a deep breath, and then she told him what she had seen. Alex nodded his head, skewed his mouth and then laughed.

"What's got into you, Jade? Is this some sort of game? People are wearing masks, that's all."

"Game," she squealed. "Do I look like I'm playing a game?"

"No, you look like you fell in the canal, panicked, and thought you saw something that you didn't."

"Look, Alex, I'm not lying about this. I'm telling you, I saw monsters."

"Okay then, show me one, and then I'll believe you."

Show him one! Was he mad? Didn't he understand? She shook her head and ran a hand across her brow. "Didn't you listen to what I just told you? They were eating people. We've got to get out of here before they come for us."

"Look Jade, you're a nice girl and all, but—"

Jade held her hand up. She didn't want to hear anymore. Her heart thudded at the thought of going back and sweat beaded across her brow, but if it was monsters he wanted to see to make him see sense, it was monsters he was going to get.

She grabbed his hand and led him through the alleys to the Rialto Bridge that connected the two sides of Venice. Down below, she could see people seated on the bank of the Grand Canal, eating meals with water lapping at their feet. She shook her head. Was everyone here crazy?

A group of people dressed in carnival attire stood on the apex of the bridge, and Jade's heart missed a beat. As she approached, she tried to swallow, but it was no good - fear had clogged her throat.

"So," Alex said, "where are they, these monsters of yours?"

Licking her lips, Jade reached out and tore one of the characters masks off to reveal an indignant woman who snatched the mask back and replaced it.

Alex laughed and shook his head. "Monsters! She's ugly, but she's no monster."

Jade blushed. Somewhere behind her, she heard mocking laughter and she turned to see a group of costumed figures emerging from the shadows.

As the group approached, a masked woman reached out and took Alex by the hand. She kissed his fingers, seductively sucking at each digit in turn.

"Now that's what I call a Venetian kiss," Alex laughed. Jade tried to force her way through to Alex, but the rest of the group barred her path. She screamed and shouted, but Alex ignored her.

The woman did a provocative little sashay. "You are fresh, yes," she said to Alex as she danced.

Alex nodded eagerly. "Whatever you say, babe." He turned and winked at Jade. "It's only a little fun. Come on, it's a party."

"They're not human," she screeched. "We've got to get out of here."

"You know what, I'm beginning to think coming here with you was a mistake. Where's your sense of fun?" He turned his attention back to the woman and started to perform an embarrassing dance of his own. "Yeah baby, let's party."

The woman took him by the hand and started to lead him away.

Jade watched as the group drifted into the shadows, and then she ran in the opposite direction.

This time, Alex was well and truly lost, but he would find his monsters, of that she was sure.

The Peacock Lawn

A mist hovered over the marsh, softening the hard edges of the landscape and lending it an ethereal, almost alien appearance.

Blowing a steady stream of cigarette smoke at the windscreen of the BMW, I tried to picture the proposed out-of-town shopping centre in this desolate landscape. There were two major landmarks, a monolithic rock and a gnarled old tree that resembled a witch on a broomstick. Shaking my head, I wondered what the hell my father was thinking, wanting to build here.

Even though the land had been in my family for generations, the local heritage society claimed it was the site of a medieval battle. Supposedly, my ancestors vanquished an opposing army, tricking them into the marsh where their heavy suits of armour dragged them down to their deaths. My father said this was all poppycock and that they had no right to tell him what he could and couldn't do on his own property. Whatever the truth, there was an unsavoury feel to the area.

The land was situated just off the M6 in Staffordshire - a prime location near a busy motorway, although at the moment it didn't even have a proper road leading to it, just a potholed trail that had made the car's suspension groan.

While pondering the conflicting issues, I noticed someone standing between the gnarled tree and the rock. Strangely, I hadn't seen the person arrive, and I frowned. The only place the person could have come from was behind one of the two landmarks. Silhouetted by the rising sun and masked by the mist, it was hard to see who it was, but I assumed it was the surveyor. Stubbing the cigarette out in the overflowing ashtray, I noticed my reflection in the rear-view mirror, my skin pale as the mist and my blue eyes ringed black by lack of sleep from worrying about the plans.

Stepping from the car, my foot sank into a pool of mud that blew a flatulent raspberry. I rolled my eyes and sighed. I hobbled to the boot of the car to retrieve the Wellington boots I wore when shooting, and struggled to pull them on, hopping from one foot to the other, cursing under my breath as I almost tripped. The last thing I wanted to do was fall over. The place smelt like rotten flesh, and god only knew what I could catch if my skin was exposed to the mud.

Walking back to the front of the car, I noticed the person had disappeared and I narrowed my eyes, scanning the desolate view.

"Hello, is anyone there?" I shouted, my voice drifting over the alien landscape and making me feel slightly exposed.

No one replied.

That was when I realised how silent it was.

The atmosphere was oppressive; I felt like I was trapped in one of those glass snow globes, just waiting for someone to come along and shake. I bit my lip, suddenly anxious. My heartbeat went up a gear.

What was it about this place? Perhaps I had listened to too many ghost stories.

The pungent aroma of marsh gas and rotten vegetation pervaded the area and I cursed my father for sending me out here. I suddenly wondered whether the gasses were poisonous; whether they could make me see things that weren't there. Combined with its history, the place certainly was spooky. But then having an active imagination didn't help.

"Hello," I shouted again. "Is anyone there?"

When no one replied, I shook my head and started walking toward the tree. I had to face my fears. Isn't that what father always drilled into me? With each step the boggy ground tried to steal my boots, and the closer I got to the landmarks, the colder it seemed to become - my breath was visible as it left my mouth, like a spirit joining its brethren in the ethereal mist. I shivered at the effects of the cold and the morbid notions conjured in my imagination.

The branches of the tree stretched toward me like claws, the witch stretching her talons. The fog swirled around me, cold and insidious.

Suddenly distracted by a rumbling noise, I turned to see the surveyor, Steve Nichols pull up in his Range Rover, which begged the question, who had I seen earlier? I looked back at the landmarks and shivered.

"You're early," Steve shouted as he stepped from the vehicle, his voice carrying easily across the desolate terrain.

"No, you're late," I said, turning and walking toward him to shake the proffered hand. "You know Mr Collins likes punctuality, so I have to be here on time to check up on you!" I winked to show that I was joking. Secretly I was glad that Steve had arrived. The area made me feel nervous and I tried not to think about the figure that I thought I had seen in the marsh.

"How is Mr Collins?" The vehement tone in Steve's voice indicated that he didn't really care how my father was.

"The same as ever."

"Still a cantankerous old bastard then!"

I pulled a resigned expression. "I know that he can be a bit of an old crock..."

"A bit. Alex, I don't know how you've put up with him for all these years. I think I would have killed the son-of-a-bitch by now."

"Well, you can choose your friends, as they say."

"Yes, but you don't have to work for him as well."

I looked toward the horizon, my lips pursed.

Steve shook his head and sighed. "You know my offer still stands. If you want, I'll have a word with a few people that I know, see what I can do to get you another job. Okay?"

I didn't even consider his offer. "Thanks, but I think I'll leave it for now."

"Does he scare you that much?"

"Are you here on your own?" I asked, changing the subject.

Steve stroked his goatee beard and nodded.

"It's just that I thought I saw someone else here earlier." I shrugged, shaking off the notion. "So what do you think about the planning permission. Are we going to get it?"

Steve shrugged his shoulders. "I don't know what your old man's thinking. Even if he gets permission to build, we will have to drain the entire area. God knows how deep that marsh is. I think this whole idea is a mistake."

I looked at the tree and rock. "You and me both," I said.

***

"How did it go?"

"Well, we c-can't really d-d-do a lot u-until we get the p-p-p ..."

"For God's sake Alex, spit it out lad, spit it out. All that bloody money on a private education and you bloody st-st-st-stutter," my father mimicked.

I blushed, always embarrassed and flustered in the presence of my father. "Planning p-permission," I said, finishing the sentence I had struggled to get out.

My father moved in circles where poise and social standing were everything; weakness was a dish from which other corporate fat cats fed. He thought that because I stuttered, I must be retarded, and he was embarrassed by me, which is why he would stop any plan I made to leave his service. He failed to understand that it was his overbearing company that caused my speech impediment. He had an assertive nature and a fiery temper that was hard to live up to. I tried my best, but my father wasn't interested.

He was a man with a voracious appetite, and money was the passport that allowed him to indulge in his second favourite passion, women.

At first, he kept his dalliances a secret, but then he started flaunting them in front of my mother like trophies, asserting his authority. Eventually my mother left. I think she had been waiting for me to grow old enough to look after myself, and in a way I felt guilty that she subjected herself to the indignity of suffering my father for so long. A messy divorce followed, with a protracted legal battle over the estate; in some ways no less bloody than the tales of yore that my father liked to dismiss.

My father steepled his hands on the mahogany desk, scowling. I looked away, embarrassed, and stared at the Rembrandt painting on the wall behind him that depicted a carcass similar to The Slaughtered Ox that hung in the Louvre. Physically and mentally, my father's strong, and the greying of his hair only added to the powerful character that he reflected. He had worked hard all of his life, building his business up from nothing, wearing his calluses like trophies.

Looking through the big bay window, I admired the lawn that stretched down to the fountain, a focal point of momentous proportions, all dolphins, mermaids and urn carrying maids spurting water. Beyond the fountain stretched the hedge maze where I used to hide as a child, knowing that no one could find me within its labyrinth passages. Peacocks displayed their plumage as they strutted across the immaculately mown lawns that stretched either side of the maze. The birds' early morning call always drove me mad; a piercing shriek that sounded as though someone was being killed.

"Well, the planning permission won't be a problem," my father said after a moment's contemplation.

I didn't doubt him for a minute.

***

As my father had promised, the planning permission went through without a hitch and my father ordered me to return to the site to meet Steve and go over the plans for the final time. It was still early when I arrived, and Steve wasn't here yet. A slight wind made the marsh grass wave as though it was alive.

The persistent mist seemed denser than the last time I had been here; I could see how easy it would have been for my ancestors to vanquish the supposed army; could imagine their screams as they sank into the mud.

Signs of action were already evident as a noisy diesel pump chugged away, draining the excess water from the marsh and carrying it along its inflated vein to a small brook a few hundred feet away. Leaning against the car, I unwrapped a packet of cigarettes and lit one, inhaling the much-needed nicotine to rid my lungs of the taint of marsh gas. Exhaling a cloud of pale blue smoke, I looked toward the two landmarks and almost choked when I saw the figure there again, silhouetted against the mist. This time the figure was waving at me, beckoning.

Puzzled, I took a tentative step forward, the marsh sucking at my Wellington boots like an insidious thief.

The figure continued to wave, but the closer I got, the less like a person it looked. Its arm contorted at unnatural angles and what I took to be a head seemed to shrink and then enlarge like a respirator. A cold chill pervaded the area and I shivered. In response to the cold, my hands began to shake and I dropped the cigarette. The glowing ember fizzled and died in the quagmire. My heart began to beat faster. Hairs rose on the nape of my neck.

Although afraid, I hurried across the marsh; perhaps the person was in trouble! The ground conspired against me, and as I got closer, the figure ducked down as though hiding and I shook my head and frowned. What stupid game was this? As I looked around, the person suddenly rose up in front of me and I stumbled back, my heart in my throat. Letting out a little gasp, I looked at the figure, my eyes wide, and then I let out a little chuckle. It wasn't a figure at all. It was a tattered black bin bag that had become entangled in the marsh grass. As the wind blew, it inflated the bag. I couldn't believe I had mistaken it for a figure.

I kicked the bag free; a gust of wind picked it up and I ducked, almost losing my balance as it sailed past me like a malevolent tumbleweed toward the diesel pump.

As I watched it roll across the ground, it was hard to imagine that I had constructed a semblance of a human shape from it.

Chuckling to myself to dispel further morbid notions, I turned and headed back toward the car. Apart from the generator, there was no other noise at all. Not even the sound of birdcall.

I had hardly taken a couple of steps when the ground began to bubble and explode with little turgid popping sounds. It was as though the marsh was alive, a living, breathing entity. Terrified that the marsh might swallow me up, I ran.

When I reached the relative safety of the harder ground around the car, I fumbled for the keys in my pocket, dropping them in the process and scrambling on hands and knees to reclaim them. A quick press of the button on the key deactivated the central locking and I yanked the door open and collapsed into the driving seat, pulling the door shut with a loud clunk. Breathing erratically, I fired up the engine, rammed it into gear and eased off the clutch. The car lurched forward and the engine spluttered to a stop as I let the clutch out too fast.

The next moment something hit the windscreen, darkening the car's interior and I let out a little whimper of fright.

It was the bin bag, fluttering over the car. I breathed a sigh of relief. In the distance, I could see the tumescent bubbles of mud becoming more frantic, as though something was beneath the surface, breathing.

Starting the car again, I accelerated down the track. I wasn't going to wait for Steve.

***

"Father, I need you to come to the site with me right away."

"Alex, can't you see that I'm busy?"

"It's important," I said, for once not stuttering under my father's malign gaze.

"What could be so important? Everything's going ahead on schedule. Now look, I've got a lot to do so..."

"But that's just it. Everything is *not* going ahead on schedule. Look, you'll have to come and see what's wrong."

"I pay other people to see what's wrong. You can deal with it. I pay you enough, so you may as well earn your keep."

"Well, I can't deal with this."

"Heavens above, are you useless as well as retarded?" Standing up, my father gave a derisory nasal snort and stormed out of the room. "Well, come on boy, I haven't got all day."

I followed him to the car with my head bowed. I didn't know what was happening at the site, and I couldn't explain what was wrong, but I wasn't going to take the blame if the building work was delayed.

Despite my father's questions, I remained silent during the journey to the site.

"So what am I supposed to be looking at?" my father asked as I parked at the edge of the marsh.

"Something's wrong over there, between the rock and the tree. You'll have to go and see for yourself."

"What's over there?" He peered through the windscreen.

I shook my head. "There's something wrong, that's all."

My father let out an impatient sigh and arrogantly indicated his leather brogues. I gave him my Wellington boots and watched him stride out into the marsh.

"You can't show me what's wrong from over there," he said, realising I hadn't accompanied him.

"I've only got the one pair of boots," I replied. "But you'll see what it is," I assured him, staying where I was.

I could hear my father's footsteps as the mud sucked at his feet; saw him falter slightly as he approached the two landmarks and I appreciated his apprehension.

Perhaps there wasn't anything wrong. I wondered whether I had imagined it. Jesus, that's the last thing I needed. Father would be furious.

Then it happened. My father began to sink into the marsh. For a moment, it appeared as though the mud took the form of scrabbling hands with congealed fingers, but it was likely caused by my father's frantic struggling because the mud suddenly regained its gelatinous consistency and sucked him down.

I watched in horrified fascination, my hands covering my mouth, as my father sank into the mud, but I was too afraid to help him. I'd heard stories about people frozen by fear, and until now, I had never believed it could happen. But there I was, frozen like one of Medusa's victims.

My father screamed, his terrified wailing reminiscent of the peacocks' cries, until the mud entered his mouth, leaving only the sound of the chuckling diesel engine.

I stared at the spot where my father had vanished. For one insane moment I thought I saw hands reaching out of the mud, scrabbling for purchase. Terrified, I started the engine and drove away from the site as if my life depended on it.

For the first few hours, I drove around in a daze. I couldn't believe what had happened.

I explained to the authorities how it was an unfortunate accident and how I tried to save him, risking my own life in the process. Obviously, it was all a lie, but I wasn't going to admit to my cowardice – besides, in a way, I felt relieved. It was as though a burden had been lifted from my shoulders. I wondered whether subconsciously I had asked my father to accompany me to the site because I knew this would happen. Perhaps I wanted it to happen. Perhaps I was just like my ancestors, tricking my enemy to his death.

The police immediately went to the site and speeded up the draining of the marsh to recover the body, and I found it ironic that the job would be completed so much faster now that my father was dead.

That night vivid dreams disturbed my sleep, and I welcomed the dawn's light as it banished the threads of the nightmare. As I rose and dressed, the peacocks made a raucous din, more raucous than usual, I thought. They reminded me of my father's screams, and I shivered. I couldn't wake up every morning and have them remind me of my father. Perhaps I would have to get rid of them.

As I walked downstairs and entered the study, the birdcalls continued. I shivered and looked out of the window to see why they were making such a noise.

It took a moment for my eyes to take in what I saw. I blinked and my jaw dropped. A squeal issued from my lips. My heart stopped momentarily and my knees went weak. I didn't realise I was holding my breath until I took an involuntary gasp, and even though the room wasn't cold, I shivered and gooseflesh erupted down my arms.

This couldn't be happening.

Fleeing the room, I ran outside toward the hedge maze, hoping to again lose myself within its labyrinth passages. As I ran past the peacocks, their screams grew louder, matching my own as I crossed the army of muddy footprints that led from north to south across the peacock lawn.

North.

Where the now-empty marsh lay.

Envy

"Is this the best you've got?" Vivian asked as she cast a cursory glance over the racks of clothes. She fingered a Christian Dior dress that shimmered in the light. "You must have something better. Everyone will be wearing this type of thing to the premiere. I want to stand out."

The shop assistant shrugged, noncommittal. "I'm sorry madam, but that's the best we have at such short notice. If we had more time, we could—"

Vivian flipped her hand, dismissing the assistant's apology. "It's just not what I'm looking for. Surely there must be something else."

The assistant shook her head.

Vivian sighed. *If I wasn't a struggling b-movie actress, top designers would be only too pleased to adorn me in one of their damn dresses.*

After a moments thought, she slipped the Versace bag from her shoulder and took out her purse. She counted out a bundle of bank notes. "Will this help you find something?" She held the money out.

The assistant looked at the money, then quickly glimpsed toward the front of the shop where the other workers were all occupied with customers. She licked her lips. "Perhaps there is something."

Vivian smiled.

"But ... I don't know," the shop assistant said.

Vivian counted out more notes. She fanned the air with them in a nonchalant manner. She didn't like being crass, but money transcended all barriers. "I'll pay whatever it takes." She only hoped it didn't cost too much.

The assistant ran a hand across the back of her mouth, smearing some of her lipstick. "It's an exclusive line. It's not yet been made available to the public."

"But it could be."

"I ... I don't know. If the owner found out ..."

"Discretion is my middle name."

The assistant looked at the money. It was probably more than she earned in six months. "OK, but please, not here. Come back when the shop's shut tonight. Ten o'clock."

Vivian smiled and put the money away. The assistant frowned.

"Don't worry. You'll get your money when I get my dress."

The assistant nodded and Vivian walked out of the shop with as much spring in her step as her Jimmy Choo stiletto heels allowed.

***

The day wore on for Vivian. She continued to shop, but her heart wasn't in it. She wondered what clothes the shop had hidden. Perhaps it was a new Jasper Conran collection, or a new John Richmond. She could see herself flouncing along the red carpet in a chiffon slip with camera lights flashing, the photographers capturing her every movement for posterity.

She glanced at her Cartier watch. Five more hours to go.

Won't this day hurry up and end?

***

Vivian stood outside the shop, trying to make herself appear as though she was just window-shopping. She checked the time again, disappointed when she saw it was ten fifteen.

Just when she thought she'd have to settle for something off the rack, Vivian caught sight of movement in the shop and the assistant appeared on the other side of the glass. She looked nervous as she opened the door to allow Vivian inside.

"We'll have to be as quick as possible," the assistant said as she locked the door, "otherwise we'll disturb them."

Unsure who the assistant was referring to, Vivian let the comment pass. She didn't think the shop owner lived on the premises. Perhaps she had misunderstood. Perhaps she meant their presence might bring the police. She allowed herself a wry smile at the thought. It wouldn't do a burgeoning actresses reputation any harm. Look at Winona. Any publicity, as they say.

With the lights off, the shop had a dreary feel, making the clothes appear drab and worthless. No easy task, considering the four-figure price tag.

Vivian followed the girl to the back of the shop. She felt like a schoolgirl on her first date and a flutter of excitement bubbled in her stomach.

At the rear of the shop, the girl produced a key and proceeded to unlock a door that was almost hidden behind a rack of Gaultier haute couture.

Vivian realised she was actually sweating. She didn't know whether it was through nerves or excitement.

"Please, try to be quiet and remain calm," the girl said.

"No one will hear us back here," Vivian said loudly.

The girl recoiled as though struck. She dashed toward Vivian, and for a moment, Vivian was afraid the girl was going to slap her. She instinctively brought her hands up in self-defence, but the girl stopped short and put a finger to her lips to indicate silence.

"The dresses will react ... badly if you alarm them."

Vivian frowned. Had she heard right? Perhaps she shouldn't have come back here in the dead of night to meet a virtual stranger while carrying a large sum of money.

"Alarm the dresses?" she whispered, more afraid that she was in a room with a maniac than of disturbing clothes.

"They're special, you see."

"I don't understand?"

"It's easier for me to show you."

Vivian followed the girl into the room. The girl's trepidation was contagious and she felt her anticipation changing to nervousness.

The room was about ten feet square and contained only one clothes rack. A collection of knee-length, drab grey dresses hung from the single bar.

Vivian puckered her lips and tilted her head to stare along the rack. She opened her mouth to speak, but the girl pre-empted her and covered Vivian's mouth with her hand.

"I know what you must be thinking, but trust me. These dresses ... they're special."

Vivian thought the girl must take her for a fool. She batted the girl's hand away and turned to leave but the girl grabbed her shoulder.

"Let me show you what I mean."

Vivian hesitated. She watched as the girl approached the dresses, and despite the dim light, she thought she saw a hint of colour suddenly infuse the material. Thinking it must have been a trick of the light, she was about to leave while the girl was looking the other way, but then another dash of colour appeared in the dresses and she gasped.

She stared at the dresses, aware she was in the presence of something truly special. From certain angles they looked almost sheer, but from others they sparkled like a pool of oil. No two dresses were alike, and, whichever way she looked at them, they never looked the same twice. One appeared diaphanous; the next minute it looked like silk. And the colours! Vivian had never seen so many colours. The dresses were like chameleons.

"They're fantastic," she whispered.

The girl nodded. "I thought you might like them."

Vivian removed her own dress and walked toward the rack wearing only her knickers and bra. She reached out to touch one of the dresses, but the girl caught her hand.

"Be gentle with it."

Already irritated by the girl's behaviour, Vivian walked back to where she had dropped her handbag. She took the money out and handed it to the girl.

"Now can I try the dress on in peace?"

The girl accepted the money. She nodded her head and moved aside. "Just remember that this dress is different. It has feelings. It reacts to things."

Vivian was hardly listening. She stroked one of the dresses, marvelling at the way the apparent warm rubber-like material changed colour and texture at her touch. The effect was almost hypnotic.

When she found a dress her size, she lifted it from the rack.

Although plain in design, the subtle changing colours made the dress special. Not wanting to ruin the effect with underwear, she removed her bra and then slipped the dress over her head. She heard the girl take a breath as if in anticipation of some dread occurrence, but Vivian had already decided the girl was not all there in the head, so she ignored her.

The dress slipped over her shoulders like a second skin and she pulled it down, surprised by how warm it felt. It hugged her in all the right places and even managed to make her bosom appear fuller and firmer, supplying the cleavage she usually achieved with a Wonderbra.

Vivian admired herself in the full-length mirror on the wall. She turned, making sure that she saw herself from all angles.

She noticed the shop assistant reflected in the mirror, her expression one of envy. The dress was perfect, more than achieving the result she desired.

The assistant licked her lips. When she spoke, her voice was hushed as though in awe. "It's a new substance that reacts to people. The designer calls them 'expression clothes'."

Vivian didn't care what the range was called - she loved it. The dress seemed to accentuate the blue of her eyes and the blondeness of her hair, while also revealing her body in all the right places. It made every side her best side and provided a flickerscape for her emotions, flushing red, orange and yellow, bright, bold and vibrant, which was how she felt.

With the aid of the dress, she was going to be the envy of everyone.

***

"So this is the dress you've been making such a fuss about," Kai said.

Vivian performed a small pirouette and the dress flashed through the colours of the rainbow. She grinned. "Isn't it wonderful?" She had adorned herself with her best jewellery, and her fingers were bejewelled with gold and diamond rings, but they paled in comparison to the dress.

Kai whistled through his teeth and nodded appreciably. "It's amazing," he said. "It's virtually see-through." He walked toward her and put his hand around her waist.

Vivian frowned. She looked at the dress and saw shimmering, bright bold colours. There was nothing see-through about it. She was trying to look demure and sophisticated! Kai obviously had a lecherous mind.

"There'll be none of that," she said, breaking free from his grasp.

Kai looked disappointed. "I would think after six months, I've earned the right to molest my own girlfriend," he said.

111

Vivian smiled when she saw the bulge in his pants. "There'll be plenty of time for that later. Besides, you don't want to arrive at your first directorial film premiere looking as though you've just fucked the star of the film."

"And why not?" He grinned, all white teeth.

Ignoring her boyfriend, Vivian looked in the mirror for the umpteenth time in only a few minutes. When she was satisfied that the dress looked OK, she said, "Come on, we can't keep my fans waiting."

***

The crowd outside the cinema was larger than Vivian expected. As she stepped from the limousine, she could feel the heat from an explosion of camera flashes. She basked in the adoration. The dress seemed to enjoy the limelight as much as she was. It radiated with bright, bold colours.

"It looks as though they like you," Kai whispered in her ear.

Vivian grinned. She could get used to this. Up until now, she had only had supporting roles. This film was her chance to shine, to put her up there with the new gods of the silver screen.

Fans were screaming. She had always promised herself that she wouldn't be one of those 'glass house' stars that don't like to mix with the public that put them where they were, but as she looked at the crowd, she thought she saw something envious in their eyes that stopped her from approaching them.

Even the security guards employed to keep the fans at bay seemed more intent on looking at her, and she found their scrutiny unnerving.

A young girl in pigtails slipped under the velvet rope and ran toward her across the red carpet. Vivian wasn't too concerned; she expected the guards to apprehend the fan, but when they didn't move to stop her, Vivian took a faltering step back, her smile changing to a frown.

Another fan slipped under the rope. Then another. Vivian shouted to the guards, but instead of stopping the fans, they started toward her too.

She heard Kai shout something, but she couldn't hear what he said above the roar of the crowd.

When the girl in pigtails reached her, Vivian turned to try and run, but stiletto heels were not designed for a quick escape. She felt the girl grab her arm and she panicked. She let out a little scream of her own. The other people advanced, and more hands grabbed at her. They pawed at the dress. Tugged at the fabric.

The barrier suddenly collapsed and the crowd pressed forward. She felt someone snatch a quick feel of her breast in the confusion. There was more screaming, but the timbre was different, borne more out of spite than adoration. She felt the dress tear. Watched as people stuffed pieces of the material into their pockets and bags. Other people crawled around on the floor, snatching at any pieces of the dress that rained down.

Elbows jabbed her ribs. Fingernails gouged at her flesh.

She tried to cry out, but the meagre air she had left in her lungs came out in a short burst that sounded like a sigh.

Vivian looked down, her eyes wide and alarmed. What little dress now hung from her body was turning red, but then she realised the colour was not part of the fabric's design.

The Times
April 21st 2006
Riot at Film Premiere

Promising young actress, Vivian Murphy was tragically crushed to death yesterday when fans that had turned out for the premiere of her latest film, Simple Minds, rioted. One eyewitness said, 'It was crazy. What did she think she was doing turning up to a premiere wearing a dress made from money and jewels. It's no wonder people ran riot.'

Reports from other eyewitnesses were contradictory. One eager fan said that she wasn't wearing anything at all. Another said she was wearing a dress made from cheap rags. And another said she was wearing what looked like a slip covered in real gold leaf.

Police Inspector Simon Rogers said, 'It seems like a case of mass hysteria. Many people claimed that the deceased was wearing a dress, but no one can agree on what it looked like. So far, all we have found are a few scraps of grey material. If anyone has any information that may help with the investigation, can they please contact their local police station.'

The case remains open.

Snake
Charmer

Rain smacked the roof of the old Ford Escort like fists on flesh. Deon Wagner stared out of the car and her reflection stared darkly back. She screwed her hands together in her lap, twiddling her thumbs.

"I don't think this is such a good idea, Simon."

Her husband tightened his grip on the steering wheel and gritted his teeth. "Look, you agreed to go along with me on this."

"I know; you don't have to remind me." She bit her lip.

Approaching an intersection, Simon crunched down through the gears, the car's engine groaning in protest as he revved the engine too high. "It's only a bit of fun."

Deon snorted and shook her head in disbelief. "You call arranging a wife-swapping party a bit of fun!"

"I didn't mean it like that and you know it."

"But I'm worried."

Simon patted her leg. "You've got nothing to worry about. You're a sexy piece of ass. Jesus, you could charm the snake out of any man's pants, and I can't wait to see you do it."

Deon's mind felt fuzzy, a sign of the sleepless nights she'd had at the thought of tonight. Looking across at Simon she saw the eagerness in his face. This was his fantasy, not hers. Their sex life wasn't that bad. Was it?

Are all men such sex-crazed monsters? Why the hell did I agree to come? she wondered. Was it to make Simon happy? Or was it because in some way she was excited by it, perhaps even a little bored of her husband? After all, he was the only man she'd ever slept with.

Her reflection continued to stare at her from the glass. Dark rings under her eyes that makeup couldn't completely conceal. Long black hair poured over her brown shoulders like oil. The plunging neckline of her flowery printed halter dress framed two crescent-shaped bulges of flesh and she suddenly wondered whether she looked cheap.

She remembered the marriage vows they'd spoken in the church, promising to be true — didn't it mean anything? From the look on Simon's face, obviously not.

They'd recently returned from Tenerife. It had been the first time Deon had gone topless on holiday. Not that she needed a tan; her Caribbean lineage showed in her dark skin. She'd been secretly thrilled by the admiring glances she received, but that was different; she wasn't going to sleep with them.

Simon was dressed in a blue casual shirt and trousers. His hair was short, mainly because it meant he didn't have to mess with it in the morning; get up and go was his mantra.

Deon thought he used the same one for sex as well.

Highlighted in the headlights of a passing car, she noticed her husband's thinning crown. They had been married for six years, and it was the first time she had noticed it. She also noticed the slight paunch that hung over his belt and the fleshy folds that had filled out his face. What had happened to the man she married? For the first time since this damn stupid idea had been proposed, she realized that the problem wasn't about her. It was her husband's attempt to prove his virility, to prove he still had what it takes.

Simon had spotted the wife-swapping advert in the local newspaper's personal column (she wondered what he was reading the personal column for in the first place). Neither couple had met before, which Simon said added to the excitement. They had exchanged photographs (her husband had wanted to send the topless ones he'd taken on the beach in Tenerife, but Deon had adamantly refused, to which he had laughed, saying, 'they'll see more of you than a few topless photos after this').

"I don't think I can go through with it. Please, can't we just go home?" Deon asked.

"Go home. Are you mad? We've been arranging this for weeks now. Look, you agreed and that's it."

Deon rubbed a tear from the corner of her eye and fished a cigarette from her handbag. She lit it with a lighter. The orange flame bathed her face in shadows, turned her eye sockets to skeletal pits.

"Do you have to do that?" Simon said.

Deon ignored him.

She switched on the car radio. 'Alive' by Pearl Jam was playing and she tried to concentrate on the lyrics to take her mind off things. But it was no good. The very thought of seeing Simon with another woman made her jealous.

Damn him!

When they first met, she'd mistaken Simon's arrogance for confidence. Now she knew better. He could be a condescending bastard. But what if he found this Tanya Black woman more attractive? What if he enjoyed fucking her more? What would she do? He was all she had.

Simon turned off Shakespeare Road and along Romany cul-de-sac. Deon felt sick, sicker than she'd ever felt. A substantial detached property came into view at the end of the road and her stomach lurched. They were here.

Parking in the drive next to a black BMW, Simon turned off the ignition and looked across at Deon. "Well, this is it."

She clenched her fists and looked down at the floor. "I don't think I can go through with it. What if we catch some disease or something?"

Simon pulled a packet of condoms out of his trouser pocket and said, "Way ahead of you." He leaned across and gave her a quick kiss on the cheek, grabbing a quick feel of her breast while he was at it.

She racked her brain for another excuse, but it was too late. Simon opened the car door and pulled his jacket over his head before rushing around to the passenger side and opening the door for her. It was the first gentlemanly act he'd ever done and she would have asked herself why, but she already knew the answer. Did he really think that was all it would take?

Deon opened her umbrella and slid out of the car. Rain pattered the material above her head and she shivered, but it was more through nerves than cold. This was stupid. She sucked at the last of the cigarette and then dropped it in a puddle. A piece of newspaper rolled past her feet in a parody of tumbleweed before the persistent rain plastered it to the asphalt. The headline read: Married to a Monster.

She tightened her grip on the handle of the umbrella, took a deep breath and walked up to the front porch. She didn't have to go through with it. No one could force her. If she was lucky, Simon would take one look at Tanya and change his mind.

She felt him give her hand a timid squeeze before he rang the bell. Light flooded the porch and she heard a bolt being slid across. As the door swung in, a woman was highlighted in the entrance, her short brown hair reflecting the light like a halo on the top of her head.

"Simon. Deon. Please, come in, I'm Tanya."

Deon's heart sank. Tanya was beautiful. How could any man not find her attractive?

Simon rushed ahead and shook Tanya's hand, his grin a measure of his delight. Deon shook her umbrella and followed him in.

She could see Simon eyeing Tanya's slim body. His gaze rested on her breasts, which strained the gaps between the buttons of the petite white blouse she had squeezed them into, and she felt a moment of indignation. Tanya's breasts were no bigger than hers, so why was he so fascinated with them?

"I'm so glad you could make it," Tanya said as she shook Deon's hand.

Deon nodded her head. She noticed the slight jiggle of Tanya's breasts and even though she hated herself for it, she felt a momentary rush of excitement. She blushed, shocked by the thoughts that ran through her head. She had never thought of women as anything other than friends, so why was she having erotic thoughts now?

As Tanya led them down the hallway, Deon could smell her heady perfume. She admired the smooth curve of the woman's thigh up to where the bare flesh disappeared inside a short, black mini-skirt. Her husband loved mini-skirts; was forever trying to get her to wear one.

At the end of the hall, Tanya showed them into the lounge where her husband, Vincent sat waiting, swirling the contents of a large brandy glass. He looked up and smiled as they entered. His hair was not quite as short as Simon's, and he had pointed sideburns that framed his chiselled jaw. His deep blue eyes sparkled.

"Glad you could make it," he said, placing the glass on the occasional table at his side and standing up to shake hands.

"It's a lovely house you have," Deon said, her voice trembling as she spoke.

"Thank you; we like to think so, don't we dear?"

Tanya nodded her head and said, "Would you like a drink of anything?"

Deon refused but Simon partook of a large whisky.

A coal fire roared away in the hearth, the flickering flames dancing up the chimney and casting an eerie radiance around the room. The only other source of light was a table lamp. The heat was stifling and Deon wiped her brow. Sweat beaded on her chest and she could feel her dress sticking to the contours of her body.

Tanya drew the curtains and then sat beside Vincent.

In the dim light, Deon admired paintings on the walls that depicted hunting scenes. Elongated horses were captured in mid flight as they hurtled hedges with beagles swarming around their hooves—the fox in the corner of the picture looked startled. She knew how it felt.

At Vincent's prompting, she sat on a long settee that curved around the wall and linked her fingers together as she resisted the urge to smoke.

The four of them talked about mundane things for a while until Vincent suddenly said, "How about watching an erotic film to get us in the mood?"

Deon gulped. This was it. Butterflies danced in her stomach and gooseflesh peppered her arms. Simon was dumbstruck for once, nodding his head like a puppet as he grinned at Deon.

Perhaps it's not going to be that bad, she thought, watching Vincent as he got up to insert a DVD into the machine underneath the television, his muscular body stretching the seams of his shirt as he bent over. The muscles in his jaw seemed to be permanently tensed as he walked toward the settee and sat down on Deon's left, the brandy glass in his hand. Tanya slid across to sit next to Simon, and Vincent gave Deon a broad smile as the film started to play.

On the television screen, a couple of young schoolgirls giggled over pictures in an erotic magazine before they kissed each other. Moments later they started to undress. The music that accompanied the film sounded as though it was being played by a tone deaf monkey on a piano. On the screen, the girls fondled each other, only to be interrupted by a young man who walked into the room. The girls giggled and one of them undid his zip, teased out his penis, and slipped it between her lips.

Deon felt herself blush as she watched the film. Although she wouldn't like to admit it, she was getting turned on and when she turned toward Simon she saw that he was kissing Tanya, their tongues exploring each others mouths. She knew she should be outraged, even disappointed that he hadn't resisted for longer, but she wasn't. The sight turned her on even more and she could feel the warmth spreading from her cheeks to her groin.

Tanya's eyes were open, sparkling with reflected firelight, and she was looking at Deon.

She licked her lips and watched Simon cup Tanya's breast in his hand. Watched as he tore open her blouse and removed her bra.

"There's one each, you know," Tanya said as Simon began to suck her dark nipple.

Deon leaned forward and gently fondled Tanya's other breast. It felt strange. She had never felt another woman's breast before. She liked it. Leaning closer, she traced the nipple with her tongue before devouring it, sucking greedily. She felt Vincent's hand slide along her thigh and up her dress to the wet patch between her legs. A few days ago she wouldn't have believed it possible that she would be leaning over to suck another woman's nipples while a virtual stranger fucked her from behind. And if someone had said that she would have enjoyed it, she would have thought them mad.

***

During the drive home, Simon was quiet, his gaze fixed firmly on the road, the glaring lights from passing cars glazing his eyes like ice. Deon meanwhile was still feeling exhilarated from the orgy that had taken place. A faint grin creased her lips on which lipstick was smeared like blood. She'd had the best sex of her life, orgasm after orgasm wracking her body with spasms of delight.

By the time they arrived home, the rain had stopped and Simon slammed his car door shut and strode toward the house without looking back. Deon quickly followed, slightly perturbed by her husband's taciturn mood. She was eager to talk about the night, amazed by how much she had enjoyed it. Perhaps it was the spark they needed to reignite their marriage. She still felt horny as hell.

Simon plonked himself down in front of the television without acknowledging Deon. He stared at the blank screen as though hypnotized, hands clenching to form fists.

"Simon, are you going to tell me what's wrong?" Deon asked, sitting on the arm of the settee and stroking his hair.

Simon looked up, his facial muscles throbbing as he clenched his teeth. "I'll tell you what's wrong," he spat, "I'm married to a whore. Worse, you don't even charge." He batted her hand away.

Deon was shocked. "I don't know what you're on about."

"You know what I mean," he growled. "Did you *have* to enjoy it?"

"Enjoy it." She was confused. "I thought that was the whole point."

He snorted. "Fuckin' whore."

"And you didn't enjoy it, is that what you're saying?"

"This isn't about me."

"Of course it's about you. It was all your idea. This was what you wanted. You've badgered me about it for weeks."

He stood up, his face pale.

Deon licked her lips, nervous. She had never seen him so angry. And seeing how hurt he was, she felt a momentary flash of guilt . . . Until he struck her, his fist smacking into her cheek.

"*Simon!*"

He hit her again, breaking her nose. Blood splattered the settee. She screamed. He hit her again. And again and again, until she curled up in a ball on the floor.

"How could you sleep with another man and woman, you fuckin' filthy dyke."

"It's your fault," she wailed. "Jesus, that's what you wanted me to do. It's not my fault if you didn't like watching it. Hell, you were so busy with that Tanya, I'm surprised you even noticed."

"Fuck you," Simon said, kicking her in the head and walking away.

The room spun around her. Pain throbbed through her body. He'd hardly ever raised his voice to her before, never mind a fist. Tears dampened her cheeks. She managed to sit up, wincing at the resultant pain.

She lit a cigarette with trembling hands, the blue/grey smoke curling around her fingers like an ethereal glove. Bastard, she thought. How on earth he's got the nerve to call me a tart and a whore when that's what he wanted me to do. I'm not his private property. A marriage certificate isn't a bloody chastity belt. She spat a plume of smoke into the air and watched it erupt like a nuclear explosion against the ceiling.

As she held her head back to staunch the flow of blood from her nose, a sudden thought came to her. She no longer loved her husband.

Actually, she hated him.

***

In the days that followed, Simon hardly spoke to Deon. He stayed withdrawn, his golden holiday tan turning pale as candle wax.

Since the wife-swapping party, Simon hadn't touched her. Not that she would have let him; she now slept in the spare bedroom.

And all the time, Simon grew more morose, not once venturing to share his feelings with her.

Deon knew she had also changed since that night. Before, sex had always been something she took for granted, Simon always willing to satisfy her. But now, forced to endure a period of unwanted celibacy, she found herself wanting it more and more.

During the day, when Simon was at work, she took to walking around the house in provocative attire: see-through Basques, G-strings, baby-doll nighties, stockings and suspenders. It gave her a deliciously wicked, decadent feeling, and it also turned her on, making her feel as horny as hell.

When the doorbell rang on Monday morning, she felt a devilish streak run through her as she went to answer it wearing a diaphanous nightie that left nothing to the imagination: it hardly covered her bare bottom. Normally she would have slipped a dressing gown on, but today she thought to hell with it. I'm a woman in my prime, and if you've got it, flaunt it. Simon could go fuck himself.

She opened the door and smiled at the blushing young man with the clipboard. He was fairly good looking, and at least he didn't have a paunch like Simon.

"Erm," he stammered, trying to avert his eyes from her breasts, but failing miserably. "I wondered if you were interested in double glazing?" He licked his lips.

"Come in," Deon cooed, grabbing him by his paisley tie and pulling him into the house. "I'm sure you can tempt me." He didn't decline and she noticed the swell of his crotch.

The salesman became the first of many dalliances. She soon found that most men were powerless to resist her advances. The hint of flesh and the sexual pout of her lips were a powerful aphrodisiac. She couldn't believe it was so easy. She liked the power she had over men, and it became a regular game to see how many she could lure into her boudoir. She even filmed a lot of her dalliances, replaying them when she felt the need. Word spread, and men were virtually queuing up to sell their wares. The wife-swapping party had awakened a sexual beast, and she was damned if she was going to let it go back to sleep.

Deep down she knew it was wrong, and that eventually she would get caught, but she wasn't bothered. Her marriage was now a sham, so it didn't matter.

Unfortunately, Simon didn't agree.

It was Friday evening. Simon had just come home. He put his work bag on the kitchen table and stormed into the living room.

"Is it true?" he demanded.

Deon looked up from her book and frowned. "Is what true?"

"That you're now the town bike, and everyone's riding you?"

"Don't be stupid."

"Is . . . it . . . true?" His voice held a menacing inflection.

She noticed that his fists were clenched. "Of course it's not."

"Don't fuckin' lie to me."

"I'm not lying."

"You're a fuckin' whore."

"Fuck you."

"Oh, I bet you'd like that, bitch."

"Get lost." She stood up, preparing to leave the room.

Simon grabbed her arm, his fingers digging into her flesh.

Deon squealed. She remembered the bruises from the last time and she regretted not leaving him then.

"You're a fuckin' slag," he snarled, spittle flying from his lips.

The words stung her like acid. What had she done? Why had she let it get this far? She couldn't believe how naive she'd been, and for the first time, she realized that Simon was right. She was being used as much as she was using.

Tears rolled down her cheeks.

"I'm sorry," she said, sniffling.

"So it is true. You dirty little tart." He slapped her across the face with the palm of his hand. "You're supposed to be my wife. How could you."

"It's your fault," she said, rubbing her smarting cheek.

He punched her in the stomach. "Everyone's laughing at me. I'd heard them all whispering behind my back at work. I knew something was going on, but when someone told me, I couldn't believe it." He shook his head. "Filthy slag."

Deon fought to catch her breath. "You didn't complain when you arranged that wife-swapping party," she said, anger replacing her fright. "You were only too glad to let another man fuck me then."

"Whore." He punched her in the face.

Deon cowered away, falling into the cabinet. She reached out and grabbed the crystal vase. The flowers she had picked in the garden fell onto the ground, and as Simon lunged at her, she instinctively hit out.

The vase made a dull clunk sound and shattered in her hand.

It was a wild, impetuous act. "Bastard, bastard, bastard," she screamed as he fell to the floor, unconscious.

***

When Simon came around, Deon was sitting watching him. Her expression was stony cold. She knew there was no going back to how it used to be. It was too late for happy ever after.

Simon moaned, shook his head, and frowned as his eyes focused on her. She watched him try to move, puzzlement and then anger showing on his face when he found that his arms and legs were securely tied to the chair.

"You know that I did used to love you once," she said.

"Fuckin' untie me," he snarled.

Deon shook her head. "I can't do that."

He looked down at his body and frowned again when he realized that he was naked. "What the fuck is going on?"

Deon sighed. "If we hadn't gone that night, none of this would have happened. It's all your fault, you know."

"Untie me, you bitch."

She shook her head. "You'll just hit me again. If I run, you'll only try to find me. That's what you're like."

"Look, just untie me. If you don't, I'll fuckin' kill you."

"That's what I'm afraid of." She picked up the items she'd gathered while he'd been unconscious and approached the chair.

"What the hell are you doing?"

"We're going to have a little fun, you and I," she said, as she began attaching the equipment to him. "See these wires? The positive one is hooked up to this metal bar."

She placed the bar in his lap. "The other one, the negative, goes to the metal ring, which goes over your prick, like so." She slid the copper ring down his flaccid member all the way to the base.

Beads of sweat formed on Simon's forehead, and a nervous twitch suddenly afflicted his right eye. For the first time, she saw something other than anger in his expression.

She saw fear.

"Are you nervous? Good. You should be. See, I've run these wires back into the garage, to the DC rectifier you have there. I have to thank you for that; you're the one who told me an AC current will knock a person to the ground, whereas DC keeps you frozen in place. It doesn't let go; kind of like you."

Deon stood up and pushed the play button on the DVD remote control. The television burst into life. The image on the screen showed her lying naked on the bed while the plumber sucked her breasts.

"All you have to do to stay safe is make sure the positive and negative elements don't touch each other."

"No! Stop! Let me go!" Simon screamed.

She rubbed the bruise around her eye, wincing at the spear of pain that shot through her.

Deon picked up her suitcases and looked at her husband for one last time. She smiled as she saw his cock already beginning to stir and begin its inevitable path towards the steel bar.

Even if he closed his eyes, she knew he would still hear her grunts and moans of rapture as the succession of men fucked her.

"This is what you wanted, isn't it? To see me charm the snake?"

She waved to him as she headed for the door.

"Enjoy the show."

Park Life

"Look at the cheeky monkey."

Following his father's suggestion, Charlie watched the Colombian spider monkey dancing behind the bars but then shook his head as though bored.

Brian sighed. It was hard work keeping his son amused. His daughter, Judy, on the other hand, loved staring at all the animals in the zoo. Brian sometimes wondered whether that was a good thing.

"I don't know…" Brian turned to his wife, Vivian. "Nothing seems to excite him."

Vivian hooked an errant strand of black hair behind her ear. "He's just young. He can't take it all in."

"What about that big lion?" Brian pointed.

Again, Charlie shook his head, then looked sullenly at the ground.

"I like it, Daddy," Judy reached for her father.

"I know you do honey." He picked up his daughter and held her to look at the lion. The beast stared back as if perusing a prospective meal. Judy giggled and pointed. When the lion roared, she roared back. Brian laughed. He could see a lot of himself in his daughter. She had the same zeal and lust for life. Charlie was more like his mother, sullen and uninterested in the park life.

"So what do you like, Charlie?"

His son shook his head and kicked his feet. "Don't like nothin'."

Brian hoped Charlie wasn't going to be like this all day.

"What about those elephants?" He pointed toward the mammoth creatures that flicked their trunks in the air.

"What about 'em?"

Brian sighed. "Nothing."

"Just leave him," Vivian said. "He'll cheer up if he wants to."

Judy waved her arm in front of her face like a pretend trunk. "I like the elephants, Daddy."

Brian waved his arm back and made a clumsy imitation of an elephant's call. The real elephants looked at him with big, sad eyes. He wondered what they were thinking.

The roar of a lion echoed through the zoo; a wrinkled hornbill took flight, the beat of its wings creating a whooshing sound like a distant storm. It landed in a tree and started making loud kak-kak noises.

"What about that bird?" Brian pointed to where the bird sat looking back at them.

"What about it?" Charlie said.

"Doesn't any of this interest you?"

Charlie shook his head.

Brian turned to his wife to vent his frustration, but she sat preening herself, imitated by a chimpanzee behind the bars. It was uncanny how alike they were.

He turned back to his son. "So what would you like to do?"

Charlie looked up at his dad. Tears welled in his eyes. "I'd like to go home."

Brian looked beyond the bars at the animals staring back and swallowed the lump rising in his throat. "Me too, son."

Defeated, he returned to pacing the well worn floor of his cage.

Meet the Author

Shaun Jeffrey was born in 1965 and lives in Cheshire, England. He lived the first few years of his life in a house in a cemetery, his playground the graveyard - perfect grounding for writing horror.

For more information on Shaun and his work, check out: www.shaunjeffrey.com

Praise for Evilution

A classic chiller from a talented new author - Guy N. Smith, Author of Writing Horror Fiction and The Dark One

Shaun Jeffrey's debut novel is haunting, disturbing and spooky as hell - Tim Lebbon, Stoker Award-winning Author of Face

www.ingramcontent.com/pod-product-compliance
Lightning Source LLC
Chambersburg PA
CBHW051927240626
47153CB00004B/1394